THE WOLVING TIME

PATRICK JENNINGS

THE WOLVING TIME

❧ ◆ ❧

SCHOLASTIC INC.

New York   Toronto   London   Auckland   Sydney
Mexico City   New Delhi   Hong Kong   Buenos Aires

No part of this publication may be reproduced in whole or in part, or stored in
a retrieval system, or transmitted in any form or by any means, electronic, mechanical,
photocopying, recording, or otherwise, without written permission of the publisher.
For information regarding permission, write to Scholastic Inc.,
Attention: Permissions Department, 557 Broadway, New York, NY 10012.

ISBN 0-439-39556-9

12 11 10 9 8 7 6 5 4 3   4 5 6 7 8 9/0

Printed in the U.S.A.   40

First paperback printing, January 2004

The text type was set in Arrus.

Book design by Steve Scott

FOR THE AMAZING LIZ SZABLA

◆　　◆　　◆

How many things were articles of faith to us yesterday
that are fables to us today?

—MONTAIGNE

◆　◆　◆

THE WOLVING TIME

The French Pyrenees

End of the Sixteenth Century

◆   ◆   ◆

CHAPTER ONE

Laszlo Emberek had spent that late-summer morning and most of the afternoon sitting under the solitary beech tree that, over the years, he had come to regard as his own. From where he sat he had a clear view over the flushing, where his flock was munching happily on fading clover. In his lap lay the half-completed, wine-red shawl he had spent the day knitting. The wool for it had come from Pernette, the flock's youngest ewe, whose coat, like the others', was the color of cream. Laszlo had sheared the fleece himself the previous spring. He'd also cleaned it, carded it, dyed it with madder root, and spun it into wool. His aim was to finish the shawl and present it to his mother at the patronal festival that Sunday. He'd not yet settled on what to give to his father.

Snoozing beside Laszlo under the tree was his sheepdog, Gizi, her long, thick, cream-colored cords spilling out onto the ground. It was just as Laszlo had decided he would take a break from his knitting and perhaps follow Gizi's example that she suddenly snapped awake and began to growl.

"What is it?" Laszlo asked.

Gizi answered with a few sharp barks, then sprang forward toward the flushing, her cords flouncing.

Laszlo set down his knitting needles and climbed slowly to his feet. He'd been sitting on the cold ground a long time, and his legs had fallen asleep. Once he had feeling in them again, he collected his crook and stepped out into the cool September sunshine to see what his dog wanted. To his surprise, Gizi did not stop on the flushing; she ran right past the flock and continued on up the neighboring hillside.

"Is someone coming?" Laszlo called after her.

Gizi kept on running and barking. Laszlo told himself she had picked up the scent of an animal, probably a rabbit, and turned his attention to the flock. "Sheep, sheep, sheep," he cooed. "Sheep, sheep, sheep."

His charges were four ewes — Babette, Claudette, Henriette, and Pernette — and the old ram, Alphonse. Laszlo lingered a moment over Babette's right flank. Her wool had been dropping out in handfuls the week before, which was common for sheep of Babette's advanced age, but now

4

seemed to be staying put. Laszlo then noted that Henriette, who often ate too much, was showing signs of bloat.

"Ease up there, girl," he said to her in a mildly reproving voice.

Up ahead, Gizi mounted the hill's crest and began to bark louder and with growing impatience.

"All right, Gizi! I'm coming!" Laszlo said with a laugh, and started up the hill.

When he reached the top, he gazed out over the wide alpine meadow, the sea of grass rippling in the breeze. The sloping birch forests encircling the meadow swayed and rustled. All was as it always was, with the notable exception of a large black wolf standing still in the middle of a patch of dried cornflowers, its dark head held up, its ears pricked.

"Go to the flock," Laszlo said to Gizi, and she ran dutifully back down the hill.

Laszlo brought his hornpipe to his lips and blew. The blare began low and wheezy, gaining strength and tone as his lungs emptied. The wolf's ears twitched as the sound reached them; otherwise, the animal didn't stir. The sheep stopped their grazing and began to bleat. Gizi growled at them and they simmered back down. Again, Laszlo sounded the horn. For quite a while afterward, the shepherd, the flock, the dog, and the wolf remained in their places, waiting for the pipe to be answered.

When Gizi finally barked the deeper woof that meant help was on its way, Laszlo turned to see a figure appearing over the horizon. It was Rita, his mother, running swiftly through the meadow, her long woolen tunic hiked up over her knees, her long black hair sweeping from side to side like the grass. She wouldn't see the wolf until she'd reached Laszlo, yet he didn't yell out. It was not the first time a wolf had approached the flock. He waited quietly, patiently, knowing his mother would soon be there and would take care of everything.

Before long, she passed Laszlo's tree and skipped out onto the flushing. She paused a moment, giving each of the sheep a rub and a coo and Gizi a scratch on the head, before scaling the hill. When she reached Laszlo, she kissed him lightly on the brow, then closed her eyes and took a long, deep breath. A strong breeze blowing in over the meadow lifted her dark hair. Without looking at the wolf, she said, smiling, "It's Agnes."

Laszlo nodded. He didn't see the wolves often enough to be able to tell them apart, as his parents did, nor could he identify them by their scents. Even so, something about the wolf had led him to believe she was the one his parents called Agnes. That he'd been right pleased him.

His mother set a hand on his shoulder to steady herself, then kicked off her wooden clogs. She pulled her tunic over her head and, for a moment, stood naked in the chilling breeze, her coppery skin taut and goose-pimpled, her body lean from hard labor and not enough to eat. Then she fell forward, her arms outstretched; before her hands hit the ground, they were paws — large, heavy, padded, and clawed. Her skin was no longer bare to the elements, but protected by thick silver fur.

As always when he witnessed his mother change, Laszlo felt a tingle of excitement shoot up his spine, as well as a pang of longing deep in his chest. He had waited a lifetime for the day when he would run wild beside her.

Rita raised her head high and locked gazes with Agnes. In that moment Laszlo sensed that a message of some sort was passing between them, in some language he couldn't understand. Then the moment passed and Rita propelled herself forward with her strong hind legs. Agnes spun around and the two wolves loped away, Agnes in the lead, Rita at her tail, until they disappeared into the shadows of the forest.

When he could no longer see them, Laszlo shot his arms into the air, one hand twirling his crook. He rose up on the balls of his feet and let out the loudest, longest, lupine howl he could muster: "Ow-*ooooooooooo!*"

Gizi howled, too, then raced back up the hill toward her master. As she reached him, the wind abruptly changed course, freezing her in her tracks. She jerked her head to the left and sniffed at the air, a growl buzzing in her throat.

"Do you smell something?" Laszlo asked.

Gizi sprinted down the hill into the cornflowers, though not in the direction the wolves had gone. She ran instead toward a distant mound of granite boulders high on a rise to Laszlo's left, to the east, a mound that had once been an imaginary castle to a much younger Laszlo. Beyond it, Laszlo spied a person — a stranger — scrambling frantically away. Panic seized him.

"Who's there?" he yelled, tearing off after Gizi. As he drew nearer, he saw that the person was small and gangly and wondered if it might be a child. "Gizi!" he yelled. "Herd!"

The dog surged ahead and in no time had overtaken her quarry. With one pounce, she flattened the stranger to the ground.

When Laszlo caught up, he was surprised to discover that Gizi had herded a girl, and a very angry one at that. She wore a filthy tunic made of coarse wool and littered with burrs and leaves. Her legs were long sticks, her feet bare and grimy, her short black hair roughly chopped, as if by dull shears. The features of her face — chin, nose, eyebrows, cheekbones — were sharp except for the blazing black orbs of her eyes. She appeared to Laszlo to be about his age, the age when one's face flames with red blemishes. Hers were made all the redder by fury. Laszlo felt sure he had seen her before in the village, and then realized to his horror that she was the girl always trailing behind Père Raoul — the parish priest!

The girl addressed him with a sneer, then suddenly leapt to her feet, clearly with a mind to escape. Laszlo dove for her legs and brought her back down. He climbed onto her chest, grabbed her arms, and tried to pin them down, but her flailing fists kept breaking free and striking wildly at his throat and face. All the while, Gizi ran around them, snarling and snapping.

"What are you doing here?" Laszlo said to the girl, just as she jerked her hands free yet again and pounded them against his chest. One blow landed at the base of his breastbone, knocking the wind out of him. As he gasped for air, the girl twisted her hips, tossing him to the ground, then was up and off once more across the meadow. Gizi bounded after her and brought her down again with little effort. When Laszlo could breathe, he caught up to them. He prodded the girl with his crook and she spun at him as if she'd caught fire.

"Don't touch me!" she hissed, swatting the crook away. "I'm not one of your sheep! And get that monster away from me!"

"Gizi, back," Laszlo said.

His dog whimpered, but reluctantly moved away. Laszlo addressed the girl again in as calm a voice as he could.

"My name is Laszlo," he said.

"I know who you are," she snarled, her eyes narrowed into slits. "And now I know *what* you are!" She squinted up at his dirty face, studied his thick, wild eyebrows, his wavy, unwashed hair, his brown eyes half-hidden behind his falling locks.

"What do you know?" Laszlo asked, trying desperately to sound perplexed. It wasn't easy. Fear had swollen his tongue to three times its normal size.

The girl didn't answer except with a glare.

"It isn't what you think," Laszlo said.

"It *is* what I think," the girl spat back.

Laszlo tossed his crook away and crouched down beside her. She shrank away, but did not flee.

"They whisper about you in the village, you know," she said, "They say you're a family of *witches.*"

The word came out like a dagger — which indeed it was — but to Laszlo's surprise, the threat had a calming effect on him. After all, she was wrong.

"People often say such things about shepherds," he said evenly. "They think because we know the names of the

10

plants and the stars that we practice black magic. But we're not witches."

"No," the girl said. "You're *gizotso.*"

Laszlo didn't know the word, or the language it came from. It wasn't French or Spanish. He'd detected an accent in the girl's voice — having one himself, he was keen to them — but hadn't been able to identify it. His only response was to shrug.

The girl made it clearer: *"Loup-garou!"*

This word Laszlo knew only too well. It was a word he had dreaded hearing all his life. It was what the French called werewolves.

He tried to scoff, but his throat had closed up. Desperately he hunted his mind for some way to convince her that she hadn't seen what she'd seen, that it had been a trick of light, a mirage, a dog, maybe, but it was no use. There was nothing he could say. She had seen and she knew *what* she had seen.

Laszlo couldn't understand how this could have happened. Rita never changed without being absolutely sure no one was around. Why hadn't she — or Agnes — scented the girl? Then he remembered how the wind had been blowing hard into their faces as he and his mother had stood looking out over the cornflowers. The girl had been on a rise far to their left, and was sheltered behind the granite boulders. It was only later, when the wind changed course and the girl fled the mound, that Gizi had picked up her scent.

"I saw what your mother did," the girl went on. "I saw her —"

"You must promise not to tell!" Laszlo blurted. "You must *promise!*"

The girl flinched at the violence of the outburst, but quickly regained her composure. She leaned forward and said defiantly, "Or else what?"

"Please promise," Laszlo said, now frantic. By asking her not to tell he had admitted that she was right. He'd let the secret out into the world. *"Please!"* he said again, edging forward.

The girl backed away. He saw that she wanted to run but that she was afraid — of Gizi maybe, or of him. Maybe she feared he, too, could change and that if she fled he would become a wolf and chase her down. He considered trying to dispel this fear, but as it was keeping her from trying to escape, he decided to let it be.

What he didn't understand was why she was there at all. Why had she come all the way from the village alone? Surely she had not defied the priest and all rules of maidenly honor — village girls were not allowed to go about unchaperoned — and traveled all this way merely to spy on him. For the first time, he noticed a small cloth satchel hooked over her shoulder, a bit of bread and some clothes peeking out of it. She was running away.

"Which way are you heading?" he asked.

She didn't answer, but from the way her eyes shifted, Laszlo could tell he was right.

"I always see you with the priest," Laszlo said. "Where are your parents?"

"In Hell," the girl snapped. "At least that's what Père Raoul says."

"They're . . . dead?"

"They're dead," she said with such flatness that Laszlo felt a chill on his skin.

He wanted to ask more questions — when? how? — but could tell the conversation was over, that she'd discuss the subject no further.

"I'll keep your secret if you keep mine," she said, her jaw set. "You never saw me."

Laszlo squinted at her. Was it possible? Could someone who had witnessed the change turn away from it so easily? What could it be that the girl was fleeing that terrified her more than the sight of a living, breathing werewolf?

"I wouldn't go up into the mountains if I were you," he

said. "You'll freeze or you'll starve, or both. Look at that." He pointed up at the clouds, which were very high and small and fleecy. "That's a lamb's wool sky."

The girl looked up, and Laszlo saw concern register on her brow.

"You never saw me," she said. She looked back down into Laszlo's eyes. "Do we have an agreement or not?"

Laszlo had no idea if he could trust her, and knew she would not last a single night in the woods. She'd be back home before morning. Would she tell? He had no alternative but to accept her terms. He extended his hand. The girl brushed it away.

"Your word is enough," she said.

"I never saw you," Laszlo said. "I promise."

CHAPTER TWO

When he arrived home, Laszlo found a lit candle, a wedge of cheese, three earthen bowls, and part of a loaf of stale bread on the table. His mother was preparing dinner. His father, Kalman, sawed at the bread with a knife, the muscles in his skinny arms pulsating like the strings of a lute. Kalman was tall and as thin as a crook. His back was slightly hunched from a life of hard work. His face was buried behind a scraggly black beard, and he shared Laszlo's errant eyebrows and wavy hair, which, like Laszlo's, was rarely washed. The family had little time or energy for bathing, and so it was done infrequently. Kalman's hands and nails, though, were scrubbed meticulously for supper.

When he'd finished his sawing, he set one hard, thick slab of bread into each of the bowls. Rita then took the bowls and ladled in the thin, hot soup. It consisted of water

Kalman had drawn from a stream, some of the few remaining leeks from the garden, half an old carrot, a tiny bit of onion, and some dried tarragon and thyme. In his bowl, Laszlo got two paper-thin circles of carrot and a few bits of leek. The broth had soaked into the bread, softening it enough to eat.

The three of them sat down on their three-legged stools, and Kalman said a short prayer of gratitude over the food. Then they lifted their wooden spoons. No words were spoken for several minutes, the only sounds being slurping and swallowing. When their bowls were emptied, they all eased themselves back from the table and rested their hands on their bellies.

"The way we gulp it down, you'd think it was actually good," Rita said with a laugh.

"It's a fine soup, Rita," Kalman said. "Fit for the king."

"*Puh!*" Rita said. "That's not saying much."

"Could I have a little more, please?" Laszlo asked.

"A glutton for punishment," Rita said.

"So why did Agnes come?" Laszlo asked as his mother refilled his bowl.

"Uncle Ugor needed help," she said with a sigh. "Poor old thing stepped into a trap. It took some work getting him out, too, let me tell you."

"A trap?" Kalman said with concern in his voice.

"Don't start fretting, Kalman," Rita said. "I'm sure it was just a poacher hoping for a boar."

"Maybe we should curtail our wolving for a while," Kalman said. "Better to err on the safe side."

"Nonsense," Rita said. "It was nothing. No one was around. Agnes came and got me and led me to Ugor. I changed and set him free. No harm done. Except that Ugor has a slight limp now." She winked at Laszlo and he forced a smile.

No one around? he thought. No harm done? Not quite.

Kalman shook his head but said nothing more.

"I met a girl today," Laszlo said without intending to. He'd promised himself he would not say a word about her. All he'd wanted to do was change the subject and it was the first thing that popped into his head.

"Where?" Kalman asked.

"On the meadow," Laszlo said. "By my old castle."

"What was she doing out there? Who was she?"

"I d-don't know," Laszlo said, realizing how foolish he'd been to mention it. "She didn't tell me her name. I've seen her in the village. She's usually with Père —"

"Père Raoul!" Kalman said, looking stricken.

"It doesn't mean anything," Rita said, patting her husband's hand. "When did you see her, Laszlo? Before or after Agnes appeared?"

Laszlo felt hot prickles on the back of his neck. Maybe, he thought, this was his punishment for breaking his promise. He'd told the girl he wouldn't mention seeing her to anyone. He considered spilling his soup into his lap as an excuse to leave the table, but it was scalding hot.

"After," he said.

"How long after?" Kalman said.

"Long enough," Laszlo lied. He definitely did not want Kalman to know what the girl had seen. Kalman worried too much as it was. Besides, the girl had promised not to tell. Hopefully she was better at keeping her word than he was.

"So what was she doing?" Kalman asked. "It's a little odd her wandering way out here alone, isn't it?"

"He didn't say she was alone, Kalman," Rita said.

"She was alone," Laszlo said. "She said she was running away." Actually she hadn't said that; he had deduced it. But suddenly the truth seemed to him like some distant country.

"Running away?" Kalman said. Everything out of Laszlo's mouth seemed to only make his father jumpier. "Away where?"

Laszlo shrugged. "She didn't say."

"I'd run away, too, if I were under Père Raoul's thumb,"

Rita said. "It must be that poor Basque girl. What's her name? Christine? Christiane? An orphan, poor girl — thanks to Père Raoul, of course."

Laszlo wondered what Père Raoul had to do with it.

"Well, we can only hope that he doesn't come looking for her," Kalman said. "I for one wouldn't like the priest dropping in for a visit."

"Oh, Kalman," Rita said. "We have nothing to fear from him. You're getting all worked up over nothing."

Laszlo swallowed hard. He knew it wasn't nothing.

"I told her to come home with me, but she wouldn't," he said. "I told her she wouldn't last long in the mountains."

"She'll turn around," Rita said. "Young people often run away, but most of them turn back the very same day." She laughed. "Oh! How's that for a rhyme! What do you think, Laszlo?"

Laszlo smiled and gave her a nod. Rita always had such a shine to her face — in her cheeks, behind her eyes. To Laszlo, she was always either laughing or waiting to laugh. Even under the direst of situations, she was at worst impatient, frustrated that laughter was so far out of reach.

They finished their soup, then nibbled thin slices of sheep cheese for dessert. It had begun to rain, so Rita put on the teakettle and the three of them moved their stools nearer to the fire. Gizi snuggled up at Laszlo's feet. While they waited for the water to boil, Rita sang a song her mother had taught her when Rita was a girl in Erdély. Laszlo loved the song and his mother's lilting voice. When the tea was ready, Rita got out her knitting. She was halfway through a scarf. Most of what she and Laszlo knitted was traded in the square in Saint-Eustache. Laszlo got out the wine-red shawl. His mother wouldn't guess he meant it for her. Kalman got out his volume of Virgil.

The family owned three books — the Bible, the volume of Virgil, and *The Iliad* of Homer — plus an assortment of pamphlets and booklets. This was more than most people had. Books were rare and expensive and, besides, few people knew how to read them. Kalman's father, Laszlo's grandfather, had been an educated man and had passed on to his son much of what he knew, along with the family's three books.

Kalman read aloud each night, reading first in the language in which the book was written, Latin, then translating it into Magyar, the family's tongue. That night he read from the *Eclogues*. Its stories of shepherds and their flocks was a family favorite.

In the middle of the eighth eclogue there came a knock at the door. It startled Kalman so much that he dropped his precious book in the dirt.

"Who can that be at this hour?" he hissed.

Rita sniffed the air. "Well, it's not the priest," she said. She set down her knitting and walked to the door.

Laszlo felt he knew who was on the other side of it, and when his mother pulled it open he saw that he was right.

"Why, hello there, my dear," Rita said.

The girl from the meadow, the one who had seen, stood in the doorway, drenched, her satchel in her hand. Laszlo was astounded by her bravery. She had knocked on the door of a werewolves' house in the middle of the night, in the middle of nowhere. Laszlo would have never believed it.

Gizi lifted her head and began to growl. "Quiet, Gizi," Laszlo whispered. The dog did as she was told, but watched the girl suspiciously.

"You're soaked to the bone," Rita said. "Come in and sit by the fire."

The girl stepped hesitantly inside, staring down at her feet.

"I'm Rita. This is my husband, Kalman, and, well, you know our son, Laszlo."

The girl lifted her head and stared at him. Laszlo believed he could read her thoughts: How did his mother know they had met?

Rita rubbed the girl's wet hair with a blanket, then began peeling off her sodden tunic. The girl wore nothing under-

21

neath. She stood naked in the firelight, a puddle forming around her feet, her wet skin contracting into goose pimples. Kalman did not bat an eye at this. The life of a shepherd — and a shape-shifter — meant he was accustomed to seeing people disrobe. Still, to help the girl feel more at ease, he stared into the fire. Laszlo, however, couldn't help looking. He had never before seen a girl his age without clothes. When he noticed that she had noticed his looking, he blushed brightly and looked away.

Rita flung a blanket around the girl's shoulders, then pressed her down onto a stool by the fire.

"Now," Rita said, sitting down beside her, "tell us your name."

The girl said nothing.

"I've seen you in the village," Kalman said, a quiver in his voice. "With Père Raoul."

The girl glanced at Laszlo, her black eyes burning hot as the coals in the hearth.

"My name is Muno," she said through her teeth.

"Muno?" Kalman said. "Not Christiane?"

"No," she growled.

"Muno is a Basque name, isn't it?" Rita said. "Short for Munondoa, yes? I'd heard that you were Basque, but then I hear a lot of things in the village. Most of the time the talk is so muffled that I can't always make out what's being said, which I usually take to mean I'm the one being talked about."

Muno's eyes narrowed slightly, and again Laszlo felt he knew her thoughts. Yes, they talked about Rita in the village. They called her terrible things in those muffled voices.

"You can live somewhere for years and years, as we have here," Rita continued, "and still remain a stranger in people's eyes."

"We are Magyar," Kalman said proudly. "From Erdély, though we haven't been there for a very long time."

"I've never heard of Erdély," Muno said.

"The French call it Transylvanie," Rita said. "I don't know what the Basques call it." She reached past Kalman for the teakettle and poured out a mug of tea. "Here," she said, handing it to the girl. "It will warm you from the inside."

Muno took the warm mug in her hands. "Thank you," she said.

"In between Erdély and here have been many places," Rita said. "Many villages, and much talk."

"My family came to Saint-Eustache when I was little," Muno said.

"I remember your mother and father," Rita said softly, and Muno's eyes widened. "I know what happened to them.

I was in the village the day they were arrested. It was unjust. Unjust and inhuman. They were young and innocent, and you were but a child."

She set her hand on the girl's shoulder. Muno blinked and a tear ran down her cheek. A heave rose in her chest and then a small cry escaped her lips before she could suppress it. It was short, but it was sharp and strong. Her body trembled as she tried to keep in the rest, but she was too weak. Tears filled her eyes. Rita knelt before her in the dirt and gathered her into her arms. Muno bawled like a baby. The rawness of it made Laszlo look away. Gizi padded over and licked at the girl's cold, muddy toes.

◆　　◆　　◆

That night, Muno slept on the fleece-lined mattress with Laszlo and his family: Rita and Kalman in the middle, Gizi at the foot. Laszlo lay awake for a long while, wondering why Muno hadn't broken her part of the agreement, why she hadn't told his parents what she'd seen. But then, just as he was finally dropping off to sleep, he thought he understood. She must have been afraid of what his parents might do to someone who had discovered their secret. She must have decided that the safest thing was to act as if she didn't know and, incredibly, bed down in a den of werewolves to prove it.

He wondered what his parents would do if they found out. Surely they'd never harm Muno. But what would they do with her? He fell asleep wondering.

CHAPTER THREE

Come morning, Muno was gone.

"I wonder which way she went," Laszlo said at breakfast.

"I'm sure she went back to the church," Rita said with a frown. "Poor girl."

Laszlo shook away a feeling of dread, then asked, "Are we going into town today?"

"Your mother and I have a lot to do here, son," Kalman said. "And you need to go out with the flock."

The sheep were always a top priority on the farm. The family relied on them for nearly everything: food, clothing, money for the tax collectors. They traded not only milk, cheese, yarn, and clothing, but also lambs. Four ewes — and Alphonse, of course — were always kept, but the rest of each spring's lambs were sold in the village square. The landlord, Seigneur Pussort, exacted a high price and it had to be paid in full, on time, and in gold. The church also demanded its tithe — one tenth of the value of everything produced each year — with equal punctuality, though the tithe could be paid in goods. The Embereks often paid it in lambs. Failure to pay these dues was punishable by imprisonment, or worse. For that reason, regardless of how much work there was to be done, the sheep were always tended to first.

"We do need some things, Kalman," Rita said. "And I have at least a dozen scarves to trade."

"And there's cheese," Laszlo added. "And I could get some fresh milk from Henriette. She needs to be milked."

"I suppose I could use more nails," Kalman said pensively. "The roof on the fold needs work before winter sets in." He shook his head. "But we can't go to town. There's simply too much to do."

"I could go by myself," Laszlo said timidly. He had never been allowed to go to the village alone before.

"No," Kalman said.

"Oh, Kalman," Rita said. "Why not? Look at him. He's so tall now, like you. His voice is deepening. He's becoming a man. He can take care of himself."

"No," Kalman said again, more emphatically.

"Please, Papa," Laszlo said. "I'll sell some cheese and milk and Mama's scarves and I'll buy you some nails, then I'll come straight home."

Kalman sighed. "Listen, son. It's better that you wait until you're able to change before facing the villagers alone. You don't know what they are capable of. Tell him, Rita. Tell him the terrible things they have done to innocent people for no reason at all."

"Don't try to scare him," Rita said soberly. "The villagers are people, remember. They are none of them the same. You know that deep down most of them are good people who are appalled at what goes on around them. It's true that sometimes out of fear or ignorance they participate in shameful, sometimes unspeakable, things. But you make it sound as if they're all bloodthirsty monsters."

"Aren't they?" Kalman said.

Rita shot him a withering glance. "That doesn't sound like you, Kalman Emberek," she said. "It sounds more like Père Raoul."

"I still say Laszlo stays here and tends to the sheep," Kalman said, trying to maintain a resolute tone, though Rita's words clearly struck a chord.

"And I say he'll be fine in the village alone," Rita countered.

They argued back and forth like this awhile longer, then, as usual, Kalman relented.

"I have too much to do to stand here arguing," he said as he stomped out of the house. Then from outside he called back, "Leave me Gizi! And be back by noon! And tend to the dung heap before you go!"

"Yes, Papa!" Laszlo said. He looked at his mother. "Thanks, Mama. I won't be gone long."

"Just long enough to see that Muno got back safely," Rita said with a knowing grin.

There was no fooling her.

"Stay clear of any trouble in the village, son," she said. "Leave if things seem to be getting out of hand, but don't fret. You'll be fine. Enjoy yourself."

Laszlo nodded, then in a small voice asked, "Mama, when will it be time for me to change?"

"Soon enough."

"Can you be more specific?"

Rita smiled. "No," she said.

Laszlo gobbled down his breakfast and ran through his chores, then he packed up his mother's scarves, some cheese wrapped in cloth, and an earthen jug filled with fresh milk and set off for the village.

The morning was bright and clear, the air so frigid, it

stung his nose. The leaves were browning and fluttering down from their branches. Autumn was making a premature appearance. The chill invigorated Laszlo, and, despite his worries about Muno — whether she was safe, whether she had told anyone what she'd seen — Laszlo walked along with a skip in his step. He passed the heavy milk jug from hand to hand and hummed his mother's old song from Erdély.

After an hour or so, small fields of rye, barley, and maize began appearing, then the small stone houses with thatched roofs and stout chimneys of the people who tended them. The houses weren't so different from Laszlo's, though of course they were utterly different; no house is the same as one's home. A couple of them were charred and roofless. The combination of thatch and hearth was a volatile one. Some of the farmyards had chickens or a pig or a sheep or two. Some had dovecotes. Every farm, though, had a dung heap, a rain barrel, a small vegetable garden, and children.

The children could be seen turning dung; building and mending fences; milking, feeding, and cleaning the animals; gathering firewood and water; and working in the fields and gardens. Most of these were boys, as the girls were kept inside to sweep, scrub, cook, and sew. A girl could occasionally be seen outside washing clothes in a wooden bucket, hanging them on a line, picking vegetables, or collecting eggs, or even working in the field. After all, some families had no sons.

Laszlo waved to all of the children as he passed, though none waved back. None ever did. They were either too busy or too tired or they had heard the whispers in the town and were afraid or forbidden to acknowledge him. Laszlo's mother had always said that he should ignore the slights of others, that he should treat those who spurn him as cordially and respectfully as every human being deserved to be treated. "'Bless them that curse you,'" she said. These were Jesus' words, and Laszlo did his best to follow them. He swallowed his pride and waved heartily at the children. Somehow it did make their slights easier to bear.

The first sign of Saint-Eustache was the church steeple peeking up over the tree line, followed closely by the sight of a wreath of stone three times as tall as Laszlo. He rapped on the gate with the massive, iron knocker and a small, square window opened. A face with a bulging red nose pressed through.

"Laszlo, my boy!" the gatekeeper said. "Good to see you!"

"Hello, Egmont," Laszlo said with a smile.

Egmont shut the little door and opened the big one. "Come in, boy," he said. "Alone, are you? Well, I guess you're old enough now."

Egmont was one of the very few villagers who ever spoke to Laszlo, and the only one who smiled while doing so. To Laszlo's mind this was because Egmont had a heart too strong to be soured by vicious rumors and a mind too sharp to believe a mild-mannered shepherd boy could be an enemy of the people.

"Busy today," he said, as Laszlo stepped inside. "This door's been swinging more than a tavern's."

He was a large man, in height and girth, but with an impish face. Laszlo thought he looked like a giant elf, as contradictory as that sounded.

"Good luck in there, my boy," he said as he swung the massive gate shut again. "Count your change and mind your purse and you'll be richer on the way out."

Laszlo nodded good-bye and walked off into the narrow, winding streets of the village. He heard and smelled the marketplace well before he reached it. What a hurly-burly! Tonic sellers hailed the miraculous powers of their elixirs; faith healers shouted "Amen!" and "Hallelujah!"; beggars pleaded and coal burners, blackened in soot from head to toe, peddled their charcoal; clanging came from the smithies, forges, and farrieries, sawing and hammering from the cartwrights' and coopers' shops; children ran about screeching and hollering, rolling hoops, playing ninepins and quoits, and chasing squawking chickens; pigs squealed, dogs barked, roosters

was Michel de Montaigne, a French writer whose work was, according to the bookseller, the duty of every Frenchman to read. Neither Laszlo nor Kalman were French, but Laszlo did not want to appear even more of an outsider to the man by saying so. He hoped his father wouldn't think that he'd been extravagant. The booklet cost him three scarves, but Laszlo had traded so well that it was really a bonus. His only real worry was that the bookseller had exaggerated the book's merits, that Laszlo had been given a taste of his own medicine. He hoped that that wasn't the case, for the booklet was to be his gift to his father at the patronal festival.

Throughout the morning, Laszlo kept an eye open for the girl who so often hung obediently behind the parish priest, but saw no sign of her. When he had been in town a bit longer than he felt he should have, he gave up and began packing up to leave. But just then an eerie lull settled over the marketplace. The clanging from the workshops slowly let up. The children all stopped their running and screaming. Murmurs swept through the crowd, and the villagers began pressing forward, toward the church. Laszlo wove through them, hopping from time to time to try to catch a glimpse of what was happening ahead, but he could see nothing. The voices rose to a chatter as the mood on the square turned restless. The animals responded with anxious whines and whimpers. The adults began to grumble and shake their fists, but Laszlo could not piece together any coherent complaint.

He had to give up moving forward — the throng had become too tightly packed — so instead he turned around and struggled back against the current of bodies. When at last he broke free of the crowd he climbed up onto a hay wagon where, over the people's heads, he could see the church doors. They were open, and standing in the arched doorway was Père Raoul, wearing the distinctive black, triangular hat — the biretta — of his calling. Instead of the long black coat he wore during the week he was draped in his flowing ceremonial robes. With his body sheathed in black fabric, his face half-concealed by the long, thin mustache and sharp black dagger of his beard, and his head topped by the black points of his biretta, Père Raoul looked like nothing so much as a black wolf, like Agnes in the cornflowers. He raised his hands high above his head and cast a censorious glare over his flock. Instantly the villagers began shushing themselves.

It dawned on Laszlo then what was unfolding. It was something he'd never been allowed to witness. Whenever his parents had sensed it beginning, they'd dragged him away. But his parents were not with him this time. Laszlo had to decide for himself what to do. He remembered what his mother had told him as he'd left that morning. Were things getting out of hand? Should he go? Could he stay?

He wanted to see what he'd never been permitted to see. Did he dare?

He leapt up and caught a tree limb, then pulled himself up onto it. He made his way through the branches to a neighboring tree, then to another, until he had a clearer view of the goings-on below. Unnoticed to him until then were four figures standing in a line behind the priest. Two officers of the court flanked them, brandishing long-handled battle-axes. The figures wore coarse, moth-eaten cloaks with yellow crosses stitched onto the front. The cloaks' hoods cast shadows over the people's faces.

"Faithful citizens of Saint-Eustache," Père Raoul said when there was quiet. "Woefully, in these troubled times, it comes too often to our attention that certain persons living among us, whether out of weakness of spirit or blackness of heart, have willingly, even desirously, given themselves, given their *souls,* to the Devil."

He paused to allow a wave of undertones to ripple through the congregation, then went on:

"As instruments of Satan, these demons bring misery and suffering to our village. They conjure hailstorms and droughts, invite injury, disease — *plague.*"

A woman cried out and then was joined by a chorus of wailing voices. Saint-Eustache, like many villages throughout France, had hosted its share of devastating plagues. All present had seen family members or loved ones felled by them. All present had also been victim to the recurring natural disasters — the hailstorms, droughts, and such — affecting the village and its environs over the years. And certainly they all had at one time or another suffered more ordinary maladies and mishaps, everything from losing a button to losing one's balance to losing a goat. In other words, everyone on the square that morning had known misfortune of some kind or other, and many had suffered it in its most severe forms, and now they began to wonder if someone — perhaps the four hooded figures before them — could be held responsible.

"These minions of Hell transport themselves through the air," the priest continued. "They bring trembling of the hands to those who try to apprehend them. They throw your children into the river and your homes into flames. They curse your fields, your livestock, your wombs, the very eyes with which you view the bounty of God's creation. They could be standing beside you, my brothers, at this very moment, plotting against you. They are among us. There are wolves in the sheepfold!"

Here, with a great flourish, he presented the four hooded figures to the crowd. The poor wretches shrank deeper into their cloaks and shook as if naked in the snow. The crowd hissed and jeered.

"But we gentlefolk," the priest said, his voice softening, "we lambs of God, we are blessed with strong, true hearts, touched by the Holy Spirit Himself, and we see beneath their sheep's clothing. We see and we bear witness, for we do not allow our hearts to be sullied, to be soured, to be sickened, by this plague of evil!" Again, his voice soared and this time the flock responded with shouted approval and amens.

"These four," he said, gesturing at the prisoners behind him, "these four have renounced God. They have entered into an unholy compact with Satan himself. For this, and for a multitude of sins and crimes committed against *you*, the good people of Saint-Eustache, these four *witches* deserve to be purified of their sins. Purified . . . by *fire!*"

The crowd roared and pumped their fists. One of the condemned collapsed and, as they were all chained together, the others fell with him.

And that was when Laszlo saw Muno. She had been standing behind the prisoners all the while, obscured from view. She wore a tunic like theirs, with the same yellow cross on the front, though her hood hung limply against her back. Her head was now shorn to her gray scalp. Her eyes were cast downward, her hands, tucked behind her.

"Come now, dear friends!" Père Raoul said, opening his arms. "Let us build a pyre!"

With a cheer, the people sprang into action. Wood was

collected and thrown into a pile, and a sturdy wooden beam was set upright in the center of it. Torches were lit, and the damned were dragged to the stake and bound to it.

Laszlo dropped from his branch and fought frantically through the mob. They were more tightly packed now, and the going was slow. When finally he reached the spot where he had seen Muno, she was no longer there. Terrified, he spun and quickly counted the prisoners tied to the stake. There were four; she was not among them. Wondering if she might have slipped away into the church, Laszlo stepped tentatively toward the doorway and peered inside.

"*Terra incognita,*" said a deep voice behind him.

Laszlo turned and found himself standing in Père Raoul's shadow.

"Oh, but I beg your pardon," the priest said with mock embarrassment. "Doubtless your kind knows not the sacred tongue of Latin. What I meant to say was, welcome to the house of the Lord, my boy, a house you are not in the custom of visiting."

"I know Latin," Laszlo said with a mixture of fear and pride. "*Terra incognita*, unknown territory. My father taught me."

The priest scowled menacingly. "Come here at once!" he commanded.

Startled, Laszlo took a timorous step forward, but then

someone brushed past him. It was Muno. As she passed, Laszlo noticed her hands were bound behind her back. She scooted around Père Raoul and took her place at his heel.

"Do not stray again, Christiane," the priest snarled. She nodded contritely, then shot Laszlo a stern glare.

"Tell your father it is your soul that is at stake, boy," Père Raoul said to him. "Yours and his and your mother's as well. Tell him that I expect to see all of you here on Sunday."

With that, he abruptly strode back out toward the pyre. Muno, trailing behind him, peeked back at Laszlo once or twice over her shoulder.

The priest raised his hands again for silence. When he had it, he yanked the hoods off the prisoners, one by one. Their heads were shorn, their eyes red and swollen, their faces gaunt and haggard, their mouths empty — of teeth, of tongue. There were three women and one man. Laszlo recognized only the man, a clog maker by the name of Paul Beart, a man not yet twenty years old, who had been in town only a matter of months. Laszlo remembered how once, weeks before, Monsieur Beart had approached Laszlo's family on the square. Being new to the village, he apparently didn't know any better than to be kind to foreigners, or shepherds. He actually shook Kalman's hand in clear view of the whole town. Then he shook Rita's and Laszlo's. Laszlo recalled the strength and earnestness of the

40

man's grip, the hairiness of the back of his hand. Black hair also sprouted from his nostrils, his ears, and his shirt collar. That, along with his earnestness, was now all shaved away.

"Look not upon them with tenderness, brothers," Père Raoul said, "for they never looked upon you with any measure of it. Rather, they have silently tormented you, cursed you, blighted your fields, your animals, the blood in your veins. This one," he said, pointing at the clog maker, "a shape-shifter, a *werewolf,* has devoured your animals. This monster has eaten your *children!*"

The crowd growled and hissed. And then a voice whispered in Laszlo's ear: "Don't turn around." It was Muno's voice. Laszlo didn't turn around. "Follow me, unless you want to see this."

"No," Laszlo said. "I'll follow."

CHAPTER FOUR

Saint-Eustache was no longer the place Laszlo thought it to be. It was no longer lively and exciting, the villagers no longer merely rude and unfair. Laszlo now understood only too clearly why his parents had always dragged him away. Who would want their children to witness such things? Then again, what *person* would want to witness such things? The villagers surely did. They had craned their necks for a better view, hoisted their children up onto their shoulders in order that they, too, could share in the spectacle.

As Laszlo and Muno wended their way through the crowd, Laszlo could not drive the memory of the victims' eyes from his mind, those haunted, gaping eyes, straining so hard for some sign of humanity in their neighbors, yet finding none. Laszlo wished dearly that he could have stood up and objected, but he knew that he was in no position to. He was not exactly a citizen in good standing. He was a shepherd, a foreigner. He did not attend church. He was shunned by even the children of the village. Standing up for the condemned would have only served to direct unwanted focus onto him and his family. Still, knowing the reason he'd held his tongue made doing so no easier to bear.

Remembering his mother's remarks about the villagers, he wondered who else among them felt as he did. How many felt the same outrage but were too afraid to speak up?

As he crossed the square, Laszlo took closer notice of the things he had chosen earlier to ignore: the prisoners in the pillories, the beggars and coal burners hiding away in doorways and under wagons, praying not to be the next to be accused. The pillories nearly always held members of this lowly caste: the poor, the decrepit, the desperate.

"*Come on!*" Muno hissed. "Stop dawdling!" She nudged Laszlo with her shoulder, and he remembered that her hands were still bound.

"Let me untie you," he whispered.

"Later," she said.

She led him through the streets to the enormous estate of the seigneur. Laszlo's heart froze as she pushed open the front gate.

"Don't worry," she whispered back at him. "The whole town is on the square."

He followed her into the gardens, past neat hedges and rosebushes and statuary. A small pool sat in the center of it with paths radiating out like the spokes of a wagon wheel. Muno ran up to a small garden shed, kicked the door open, and beckoned to him. He ducked inside behind her.

"Now," she said, "cut me loose."

Laszlo picked up a pruner and snipped through the hemp cord binding her wrists. She shook blood back into her fingertips.

"Now help me clear this away," she said, and began moving aside tools and pots. Laszlo helped her, then together they slid away a large wooden crate, revealing a trapdoor in the floor. Muno swung it open. A dark tunnel led straight down into the earth. A ladder leaned against its wall.

"Stay close," Muno said as she lowered herself down.

Laszlo followed her. The air in the tunnel was cold and damp.

"Hold my hand," Muno said when they had reached the bottom. "I know the way."

Laszlo did as she said and she pulled him through the dark until they emerged through another trapdoor, which was obscured by a tangle of juniper. They were outside the village gate.

"Let's keep moving," Muno said.

"Where to?" Laszlo asked.

"I don't care," she said. "Away."

"You're running away again?"

She didn't answer, but didn't need to. Laszlo felt a shiver of fear, realizing she was so openly defying a man of such terrifying power as Père Raoul.

"I was supposed to be home hours ago," he said. "Follow me there."

Muno grudgingly agreed. Laszlo glanced once over his shoulder as they ran down the path and saw dark smoke rising up in a column through the trees, high into the clear sky. He did not look back again.

◆　◆　◆

Kalman did not say a word about Laszlo's lateness. The sight of the yellow cross on Muno's tunic had rendered him speechless. He knew the mark of the heretic well. Laszlo handed him the nails, then slipped away to the house before Kalman could muster words of complaint. Inside, Laszlo handed his mother the needles, coins, and remaining scarves, then slid the booklet he'd bought for his father deep into a basket of unspun wool. He collected his knitting and stuffed it in his pocket.

"Is that for running away?" Rita asked Muno, pointing at the cross on her chest.

Muno nodded.

"And yet you're out here again?"

The girl stared at the floor.

"Come on, Muno," Laszlo said, hustling her away. "Papa wants me to get the flock out to the flushing, Mama." Lying was becoming second nature to him.

As they hurried toward the sheepfold, Muno whispered, "You didn't tell them what happened today."

Laszlo shook his head.

"I'm surprised," she said. "I thought you told them everything."

There was no mistaking what she meant by that.

"I'm sorry," Laszlo said without looking at her.

"It doesn't matter. Your parents are kind. They wouldn't have told anyone."

"Did you tell anyone?" Laszlo asked apprehensively.

"No," she said. "I keep my word."

The sheep were nearly as glad to see Laszlo as he was to see them. Standing among them, pressing his hands into their fleece, hearing their happy bleats, helped him to drive away the hideous images of the morning and begin to feel good again about being alive on such a sunny day. When Gizi ran up and licked his face, Laszlo couldn't help but smile ear to ear. Gizi licked Muno's face, too, though she wasn't as happy about it.

"I know she's a sheepdog," Muno said, "but did you actually cross a sheep with a dog?"

"She's a puli, a Magyar sheepdog," Laszlo said. "I think the sheep trust her because she looks like them. Sheep aren't very trusting of dogs in general."

"How do they feel about your mother?"

Laszlo didn't answer. It wasn't a respectful remark. He tied a lead around Alphonse's neck and led him out of his pen.

"This way we won't have to keep stopping along the way," he said. "Alphonse is old, but he still mounts the ewes one right after the other. We're not sure he settles them each time, so we let him try as much as he's able. And he's still pretty able."

Suddenly realizing what he was talking about, Laszlo's ears and cheeks turned bright red. Neither he nor Muno said another word until they were sitting under the lone beech tree on the flushing. Laszlo took out his knitting.

"That was the first time I've ever witnessed . . ." he began, but could not finish.

"It wasn't mine," Muno said, twirling a blade of grass between her fingers.

Laszlo peeked over at her. He had to know.

"Your parents?" he asked.

Muno didn't respond, but the answer was written on her face.

"Was it Père Raoul?"

"One day he'll tie me to the stake, too," Muno said in a brittle voice. "He says the Devil is in me just as it was in them."

"Are you his prisoner?"

"More like his slave. He says he's saving me, 'setting me back on the path to righteousness,' 'cleansing my soul.' I do most of the cleansing, though. I scrub the floors morning to night."

Laszlo saw that her hands were blistered and chapped, and her knees rubbed raw.

"Do you think he saw us leave together?" he asked.

"I'm sure someone did. There will be talk. He made me swear that I would not leave his side."

Again, the flatness of her tone gave Laszlo a chill. How could she be so nonchalant about such grave matters?

"Then why did you lead me away?"

"I wanted to talk to you."

Laszlo was too afraid to ask why.

"Père Raoul has heard the whispers."

"The whispers?" Laszlo said, fear creeping up his neck.

"Yes. I heard him discussing your father this morning with members of the Fabric. Isn't your father's name Kalman Emberek?"

Laszlo couldn't breathe.

"You must all leave immediately," Muno said. "Go far away."

"Go? Leave our home?" Laszlo couldn't stand the thought of it. He couldn't imagine living somewhere else, someplace that wasn't his home. "But why? What are people saying?"

"That you don't go to church," Muno said. "That you speak with an accent. That your eyebrows meet. That you practice black magic."

Laszlo's fear spread. "Have we been *denounced*?"

"I don't think so, but you can't stay long enough to find out."

"But Père Raoul spoke to me today," Laszlo said. "He asked me to bring my parents to church. Why would he do that? Why didn't he arrest me?"

"Maybe he wants to lure you all into town," Muno said.

"But he knows where we live," Laszlo said. "He could come out and arrest us anytime he liked. Or he could arrest us in the village when we come in to trade."

"Listen to me," Muno said. "If the priest believes you are

heretics, your lives could be destroyed. Even if you aren't burned alive at the stake, you will lose everything — your house, your clothes, your animals."

"He'll take Alphonse? Babette? Gizi? *Why?*"

Muno shook her head. "He will put you in the dungeon and you'll never see the sun again. He'll torture you and he'll torture your parents. He believes all witches know other witches and he'll torture you until you give him names."

"But we don't know any witches!"

"Then you'll be tortured for a very long time. You'll be tortured until you say whatever he wants you to say, until you give him a name, any name, and then that person's life will be destroyed, too. Those three women today had been in his dungeon for years. Couldn't you see it in their faces? The man who was burned was denounced by one of them. The woman had never set eyes on him before. Père Raoul believed that the man could change into a wolf. Why? Because he was hairy, and because he was a stranger. So he had the woman tortured until she said what he wanted her to say.

"The man had no idea what Père Raoul was talking about when he was arrested. It can happen that fast, without warning. They asked him for names, too. He didn't have any, so he was tortured. They sat him on a metal stool and set a fire under it. After that, they hung him up by his feet and hands and tied weights to his ankles and wrists. One of his arm bones shattered." She closed her eyes. "He's better off now."

"Did he ever give a name?" Laszlo said, remembering how the man had shaken his hand.

"You have to leave," Muno said. "It may already be too late."

Laszlo opened his mouth again to speak, but nothing came out. He had more questions but he did not want to hear more answers. Instead, he stood up and walked out among his flock. Babette's wool was falling out again, from worry, no doubt. When Laszlo fretted, so did she.

"It's all right," he whispered to her. She nuzzled into his hand. He turned to Muno. "The sheep are happy here," he said.

She peeked over at Alphonse, who was mounting Claudette.

"So I see," she said with a cocked eyebrow.

Laszlo blushed.

"Tell me," Muno said, "that wolf, the one that came here that day, the one your mother ran away with, was it a . . . ?"

"No," Laszlo said. "Agnes is a wolf. She doesn't change."

"Agnes?"

"That's what we call her. We give the wolves names. Magyar names. They don't understand them, of course. We do it for our benefit, so we can talk about them."

"The wolves are your friends?"

"Some of them. Agnes and her mate, Fridrik, and their pack are our neighbors."

"You're not afraid of them?"

"They'd never harm us," Laszlo said. "Our families have a kind of pact. We look out for one another. Besides, my parents say wolves don't prey on people."

"You'd have a hard time convincing anyone in the village of that."

"They don't say no wolf has ever attacked a human being," Laszlo said. "They say that usually when a wolf attacks a person it's because the wolf is sick, or desperate. There are many wolves that don't have enough to eat because either their prey has been decimated by humans or members of their pack have been killed by wolf hunters, which makes it more difficult to bring down big game. It's never easy making a living in the wild and these extra hardships sometimes cause a wolf to do things it normally wouldn't do.

"And then some wolves are just aggressive, the way some people are. Wolves have different personalities just like people. My mother says people often make the mistake of thinking every person is unique, but that all animals are the same: all ravens act the same, all bears, all wolves. But they don't. Every wolf is different."

"So wolves aren't killers?" Muno asked.

"No, wolves kill," Laszlo said. "But they don't kill out of fear or anger. They respect the lives they take. They know they rely on them for their survival. Wolves aren't cruel. They don't have dungeons or pillories. They don't burn their own kind at the stake. They don't torture the innocent. They may sometimes prey on human beings, but so do people. People prey on everything, including themselves. It's people I'm afraid of."

"I'm a person," Muno said.

"And I'm afraid of you."

Muno smiled slightly. It was the first time Laszlo had seen her do so.

"I suppose I should be afraid of you, too," she said.

"I was surprised you came to our house," Laszlo asked. "Weren't you afraid?"

"There are scarier things in the world than seeing a person turn into a wolf," Muno said. "I've seen people turned into slaves. I've seen them turned into living skeletons. I've seen them reduced to ashes. All I know about werewolves is that Père Raoul says they're evil. From what I saw, your mother looked like a kind person. The way she stopped and patted the sheep and your dog, the way she kissed you and rested her hand on your shoulder. There was tenderness in it. Then she changed, and I thought, well, Père Raoul is wrong again. Who is he to judge evil, after all?"

"Then why did you run?" Laszlo asked. "Why did you fight so hard when I caught you?"

"I ran because your dog started barking. I didn't want to be caught. I wasn't supposed to be there."

"Why didn't you just pretend you hadn't seen my mother change?"

"Would you have believed me?"

"No, I guess not."

"I wasn't afraid of you. I'm not afraid of anything. When it started to rain, I had no place to go. So I went to your house, the lair of the werewolf."

"My parents are werewolves. I'm not." Laszlo had never admitted that to anyone before. It was both terrifying and liberating at the same time. "But one day I'll be one, too," he said.

"When?" Muno said, her black eyes opening wider.

"I don't know. They keep telling me it'll be soon."

"How does it happen?"

Laszlo shrugged. "I won't know until it's time."

Muno nodded slightly, her gaze still hard upon him.

"Are you afraid of me now?" Laszlo asked.

"Should I be?"

"No."

"Then I won't be."

"I'm still afraid of you," Laszlo said.

Muno grinned. "You should be."

CHAPTER FIVE

"Why was she wearing that cross?" his father asked that night at the table.

"It was only for running away, Kalman," Rita said, ladling soup over slabs from the same loaf of bread, now a day older.

Laszlo confirmed this with a nod.

"That girl's parents were burned as witches," Kalman said. "She's branded. Associating with her could be very dangerous."

"Kalman," Rita said sharply. "Don't whip yourself into a panic. And don't discourage Laszlo from seeing Muno. She's the first real friend he's made here."

"We have to be realistic, Rita," Kalman said. "Condemnation rubs off. It all starts with a whisper."

The word sent a shiver down Laszlo's spine. He wanted

so much to tell them what Muno had seen on the meadow, about what she'd heard Père Raoul say. It was torture keeping it in. But he couldn't. It would mean losing everything he loved: his home, his hills, and . . . Muno? Was he keeping all this from his parents because he didn't want to be sent away and never see her again? That was impossible. How could she be that important to him in so short a time? He'd pled with her that afternoon to stay, but she wouldn't; she returned to the village, to Père Raoul. Since then Laszlo hadn't been able to stop thinking of her, worrying about her. How could that be? He barely knew her.

"I still think we should be very careful," Kalman said. "We need to pay attention to little things like traps and yellow crosses. Our kind has to be eternally on guard."

Our kind, Laszlo thought. That was what Père Raoul said: "your kind." What did he mean by that? Did he mean shepherds? Peasants? Magyars? Or did he mean something else?

Muno said she'd heard him talking about Kalman. Maybe what he'd been saying was that he'd never seen the family in church. Maybe that was all he wanted. Maybe he wanted Laszlo and his parents to go to church in order to dispel the rumors circulating about them. Surely, as a man of the cloth, his chief concern was in keeping people in the fold, keeping them pious, not condemning innocent, Bible-reading people to the stake. Unless Muno had told him, he'd have no reason to suspect the truth about what they were. Laszlo was skeptical of Muno's suggestion that the priest had instructed him to bring his parents to church under false pretenses. Père Raoul didn't need to set a trap. If he wanted them arrested, there was nothing to stop him. Laszlo decided that the best thing he and his parents could do would be to accommodate the priest.

"I think we should go to church on Sunday," Laszlo said into his bowl.

"Whatever for?" Rita laughed.

"I don't know," Laszlo said, pretending it was an innocent, impetuous idea. "Maybe it would show everyone that we believe in God."

Kalman scratched his beard, mulling this over. "You may be right, son," he said. But then he shook his head. "No, I don't trust Père Raoul. And I don't trust the church. I've seen too much of its handiwork."

Laszlo knew that this was the reason the family never attended mass. It wasn't that they weren't devout. Laszlo's parents simply couldn't abide the church's awful ministrations.

"You know, maybe we ought to go," Rita said. "This Sunday is the patronal festival. It could be fun."

"Fun," Kalman grumbled.

"Yes, fun," Rita said. "Everyone's entitled to some now and again."

Kalman grumbled again.

Laszlo wished to himself that his mother's powers of persuasion were as effective as usual, for if they went to church that Sunday, there was a chance he might see Muno again.

◆　　◆　　◆

On Sunday, the three of them sat side by side on a wooden pew in the stone church of Saint-Eustache. Rita proudly wore her new wine-red scarf. Kalman carried in his pocket the pamphlet Laszlo had given him. He'd been so excited by the gift that he'd neglected to ask Laszlo how he'd procured it. Laszlo wore a brand-new hemp cloak, a present from his parents. It was clean and without holes and, for once, Laszlo felt almost presentable. He hoped that Muno would see him in it, but upon recalling the wretched garments she was forced to wear, thought better of it.

Kalman opened his Bible across his lap. He was one of the few in attendance who had one, and he hoped that the sight of a shepherd who'd made the necessary sacrifices to own one would allay any doubt of the family's piety. He flipped to Isaiah, and pointed to a passage that Laszlo knew by heart:

> The wolf shall dwell with the lamb,
> The leopard shall lie down with the kid,
> The calf and the lion and the fatling together,
> And a little child shall lead them.

The crowd shushed itself as Seigneur and Madame Pussort entered the church through their private door. The seigneur wore a jerkin of green silk over his doublet, with a great white ruff around his neck. On his head he wore a black felt cap with a white hawk feather sprouting out of it. Over his shoulder a golden baldric supported his glistening, finely engraved sword. His beard, like the priest's, tapered downward like a blade, his thin, waxed mustache providing the hilt. He doffed his cap and made the slightest of bows to those assembled, who sat motionless, gazing up at this exquisite, honorable, gracious man, the owner of most of the town, including the church in which they sat, the man who took most of their earnings and gave precious little in return. They gaped at the fine gown and glittering jewels of the man's wife who lived with her husband in a castle with servants and horses and a carriage and herds of livestock. The couple strode regally by, then, with a flourish of cape and gown, took their seats beside the pulpit. Their eyes gleamed in the light of the many candles set before them. Those gathered gazed upon them with reverence in their eyes, but resentment in their hearts.

Père Raoul appeared next through the church doors, at the back of the congregation, adorned in his black ceremonial robes. The crowd twisted around. To Laszlo's disappointment, Muno was not trailing behind him. Laszlo watched as the priest moved solemnly up the aisle, swinging a smoking censer. The strong scent of incense began to drown out the stench of the attendees, which, in such concentrated quarters, was strong indeed. Père Raoul assumed his place at the front beside the lord and his lady, and the mass began.

During it Père Raoul spoke, in Latin, of Placidus, a Roman general who saw an image of Jesus Christ on the cross in the antlers of a stag. Placidus, Père Raoul said, was subsequently baptized, along with his wife and two sons, and took the name Eustache. Later, the stag appeared to him again, this time foretelling disaster. Soon afterward, Eustache's home was robbed. His beloved horse and all of his servants mysteriously fell dead. In an attempt to flee to Egypt, Eustache and his wife were separated, and their sons were carried off, one by a lion, the other by a wolf. The boys were later rescued by some good-hearted farmers and shepherds, and Eustache and his wife were reunited. The Roman emperor promoted him in the army. However, when Eustache refused to worship the Roman gods he was thrown, like any Christian, to the lions. He emerged unharmed, though, when, to everyone's amazement, the lions became inexplicably tame. Enraged, the emperor ordered that Eustache and his family be put inside a brass bull, under which a bonfire was set. All four of them perished, though it was widely maintained that their flesh did not burn.

"Eustache," Père Raoul said, "became the patron saint of hunters. Today we honor his goodness, his vision, and his memory."

Laszlo didn't know what to make of the story. Eustache was a hunter saved first by his prey, then by the wild beasts dispatched to kill him, and yet he was the patron saint of *hunters*, of men who kill animals. It didn't make any sense.

When at long last Père Raoul concluded the mass, the villagers — nearly all of whom did not understand a word of Latin — streamed happily from the church. It was time for the festival to begin.

Seigneur Pussort, Père Raoul, the members of the Fabric, the curates, and the wealthy merchants of the town (the miller, the baker, the vintner) took their places at a long table near the church doors and sampled wines from its cellars and dined on partridge prepared by the seigneur's chef.

The peasants ate the food they themselves had brought, mostly stews with bits of pork or ham and stale loaves of bread, and drank plenty of their own fermented cider. Then they danced and drank some more. By the afternoon, fights had started breaking out. Laszlo and his parents would have left after the service except that Kalman wanted to linger long enough to try to pick up any gossip from the drunken (and so less inhibited) revelers, and because Rita wanted to dance. As Kalman was busy with his eavesdropping, she danced with Laszlo.

Laszlo searched the crowd for Muno as his mother spun him around and around. He feared that she was in the church dungeon and tried not to allow himself to consider what that might mean, though an image of her being led to a hot metal chair kept appearing before his eyes. He shook it away again and again and tried to give in to the gaiety all around him.

And then he saw Père Raoul standing at Kalman's elbow. "Mama!" he whispered. *"Look!"*

Rita glanced over, then in a loud voice said, "I think I'm tiring, dear son! I'm not as young as I used to be! Where is your father?"

"There he is!" Laszlo said, going along with the pretense, and they skipped over to where Kalman and the priest stood together talking.

"No, your grace," Kalman was saying. "It's not for lack

of devotion that you have not seen us at church. I am a shepherd, sir. I come from a long line of them, I'm afraid. In fact, my ancestors were all set into their coffins with tufts of wool stuffed into their cold hands. That way, St. Peter would know their vocations and excuse them for not attending mass." He smiled his humblest smile.

"I excuse you now, my son," Père Raoul said with a polite laugh. "But I do hope to see you again next Sunday." He turned to Rita, bowed, and said, "Blessings, madame." Then to Laszlo he added, "I commend you on your powers of persuasion, my boy."

At first Laszlo didn't understand, but then it occurred to him that Père Raoul was probably referring to the family's presence at church. Still, Laszlo couldn't help feeling that Père Raoul was insinuating something more, perhaps something to do with Muno, maybe something Laszlo had persuaded *her* to do. But what? And then he thought he knew: he had persuaded her not to tell. If Père Raoul knew about the persuasion, did that mean that Muno had told him what she had seen? Had Père Raoul tortured her into telling? Or was he commending Laszlo because he could *not* get Muno to talk? Laszlo had no way of knowing, which unnerved him terribly.

"And where is your little girl today?" Rita asked with a bright, false smile. "She isn't tucked into your robes as usual."

The priest's congeniality fell away. He stared at Rita with a gimlet eye. She pretended not to notice.

"Sadly, poor Christiane is ill," Père Raoul said, taking on an air of deep concern. "She has taken to her bed with a fever."

"Oh, dear!" Rita said. "I hope it isn't anything serious! So many have been swept away from us by these dreadful mortalities."

"I invite you to join me in praying for her, madame," the priest said, pressing his palms together.

"I will," Rita said with mock graveness, then added, "but excuse us now, Father, for my husband has promised me this dance!" She hooked Kalman's arm, grasped Laszlo's hand, and pulled them both away.

Once they were back among the dancers, Kalman scolded her, but Laszlo could only marvel at her courage. Rita goaded and teased Kalman until his anger dissipated and he reluctantly began to dance. He even smiled, and then later became almost giddy, clapping and twirling to the music of the band. And that was when they saw it. It seemed to catch the attention of all three of them at once.

Across the churchyard, hanging from a post, stretched and bound to a makeshift wooden frame, was the hide of a black wolf. There were the paws, the tail, the head, the holes where the eyes had been. No two wolves, like no two people, ever look alike; every pelage has its own distinctive markings. The hide was Uncle Ugor's.

◆　◆　◆

"It was wrong, criminally wrong," Rita argued as they walked home, "and it deeply hurts. Ugor was a kindhearted soul whom I loved very much." Laszlo noted a catch in her voice as she said this. "But we have no reason to worry. There is absolutely no connection between this and us. And today we got into the priest's good graces."

"With no thanks to you," Kalman said. "Why would you ask about Muno? Are you mad? You certainly succeeded in arousing his suspicion, if that was your intention."

"Oh, he's such an old bore," Rita said. "Besides, you won him over. That tuft-of-wool story works every time." She turned to Laszlo. "Your father has trotted that one out for every clergyman he's ever met."

Kalman couldn't help but grin. "It is good, isn't it?"

Rita pinched his cheek. "Yes, shepherd boy, it's good."

Laszlo could tell Rita would convince Kalman that they'd be safe staying, if she hadn't done so already, but found no real peace in the thought. The specter of Uncle Ugor skinned and drawn and displayed was not easy to dismiss, and things were worse than Kalman knew. This time, his worries were well-founded. Even so, Laszlo wanted to stay. He couldn't leave now. Muno wasn't ill, as Père Raoul had said. She was in trouble, and somehow Laszlo was going to have to help her. Hopefully he could do so without jeopardizing his family in the process.

By the time the farm came into view, Kalman had relented. They would stay, though on the condition that a moratorium on wolving must be observed.

"After we visit Agnes and Fridrik," Rita said. "We need to offer our condolences."

"Yes," Kalman said.

Then from ahead they heard the flock begin to bleat, then Gizi to bark.

"Something's wrong," Laszlo said.

The three of them raced toward the fold and were met by Gizi at the gate. She barked louder and circled anxiously around them.

"Calm down, girl," Laszlo said. "What is it?"

"There!" Rita said, shading her eyes with her hand and pointing out across the meadow.

Laszlo squinted into the setting sun and, in the distance, made out the dark silhouette of a wolf.

"I don't recognize him," Kalman said.

Rita sniffed at the air. "Nor do I."

They both peeled off their clothes, fell forward, and were

67

wolves. Kalman was silver like Rita, but larger, and with a spray of white fur below his deep, brown eyes. Rita had smudges of copper fur curving over hers. The two of them loped out across the meadow toward the stranger, leaving Laszlo standing beside two piles of clothes. He let out a deep sigh, longing for the day when he could go with them. *Soon,* he told himself, *soon.* He was tired of the word.

The black wolf growled as Kalman and Rita approached. Rita hung back while Kalman circled him a few times, marking his territory. Then Kalman raised his tail and hackles, arched his back, stiffened his legs, and edged in closer. The stranger immediately flipped onto his back, tucked his tail between his legs, and exposed his throat. Kalman walked stiff-leggedly up to him and pressed his snout in close. The black wolf licked it. He had submitted.

Kalman relaxed then and sauntered around him, his head held high. Though he was an adult, the black wolf behaved much like a puppy, frolicking in the grass, whining for attention. Rita moved in and the wolf regarded her as he had Kalman: deferentially. When Kalman and Rita led him away in the direction of the woods, the wolf remained in his place at the rear.

"Must be a lone wolf," Laszlo whispered to Gizi. "They'll take him to Agnes and Fridrik."

He scratched Gizi's head and told her she was a good

dog, then went into the pen and patted the ewes and spoke to them in low tones until they had quieted down. He checked Babette's wool and, again, it came out in his hands. He checked her teeth. There was another loose one.

"You're not well, old girl," he said sadly.

She nuzzled into his leg.

Laszlo then went into the house and took out a knife and sliced a piece off a wheel of cheese. He ate half and tossed the rest to Gizi. Then he got to work starting a fire. Once it was kindled he filled the soup pot with water and hung it on its hook over the fire. He chopped up what few vegetables he could find. There weren't many, but he was too tired to go out to the garden to collect more. He doubted there was much out there, anyway. He threw the vegetables into the pot with some herbs and began to stir. This whole process of doing something mundane and useful soothed his worries. He pulled up a stool to the hearth and sat down. Gizi curled up beneath it. Within moments Laszlo's eyelids had slid shut.

A sudden sound outside shook him awake — the sound of a stick being snapped in two. Gizi growled. Laszlo went to the paneless window and peered out. Darkness was falling and the meadows glowed with an eerie blue light.

The family didn't own a proper weapon — no gun, not even a bow. The only things in the house Laszlo could use to defend himself were the kitchen knife, the wool shears, his crook, and some knitting needles. The knife was closest at hand.

"Who's there?" he shouted, though he was not foolish enough to believe that someone intending him harm would reply. Gizi barked and then Laszlo saw a dark shape dash between the dung heap and a tree. The shape was upright — a person. Laszlo gripped the knife handle tighter.

"I'm armed!" he said in a deep voice.

The figure darted from the tree toward the fold, and Laszlo hollered, "Stop! I'll fire!"

The figure froze.

"Don't!" a frail, female voice answered. "Please!"

She stepped forward, and Laszlo saw that she wore a tunic with a yellow cross sewn onto the front.

He dropped the knife and ran out the door toward her. She buckled at the knees as he reached her and fell into his arms. She was as light as a lamb. He eased her down, cradling her, her face pressed into his chest.

"Muno," he said, the word coming out more a sob than a name, and her head turned and her eyes gazed up at him. They were pale eyes, blue eyes, not the eyes he was expecting.

"She's in the dungeon," said the woman — for that was what she was, a woman. "She helped me to escape."

Laszlo felt awkward holding a strange woman, a fugitive, in his lap. He held her nonetheless.

She was older than Muno. Laszlo guessed she was as old as thirty. She had the same fragile emaciated look as the four prisoners on the square. Laszlo wondered how much of her life she'd lost to the dungeon.

"Muno told me about you," she went on, each word slow in coming. "She told me that if you were still here you might help me."

"Of course," Laszlo said uncertainly. He couldn't fight the feeling that he was inviting more trouble into his life.

The woman smiled weakly. "Your secret is safe," she whispered, her head lolling back, her eyes filling with tears. "Muno told me to tell you that."

CHAPTER SIX

Laszlo brought the woman inside and wrapped her in one of Rita's shawls. He served her cheese, which she devoured ravenously.

"I put soup on," he said, "but it isn't very hot. Would you like some anyway?"

The woman nodded politely. Laszlo started sawing at the loaf.

"I should get the ax," he said, trying to smile.

The woman tried to smile back, but she was too out of the habit and it came out looking like a wince.

When Laszlo had finally sawn off a slab of the bread, he set it in a bowl, then ladled some of the broth over it. The woman cupped the bowl in her hands and inhaled deeply.

"It's just water with a tiny bit of onion and carrot," Laszlo said. "It's all we have."

The woman didn't reply; she was already slurping at the warm liquid. Soon she had drained the bowl. Laszlo refilled it.

"I tried to convince Muno to come with me," the woman said, "but she said the priest would surely send out a search party for her, while he might not for me. They don't always look in on each prisoner every day, so perhaps they haven't yet noticed I've gone. But Muno knows they would miss her in a minute. She told me to tell you not to worry, though, that she'll escape when the time is right. She knows where all the secret doors and passageways are, and where the keys are kept."

Laszlo remembered their escape through the seigneur's garden shed.

"She told me to tell you that under no circumstances are you to attempt to rescue her or even to inquire about her. That would only make matters worse for everyone. She said she hoped you wouldn't still be here, but that if you were, you might help me. I'm glad you're still here." Again she tried to smile, this time more successfully.

Under the firelight Laszlo saw that she was not as old as he'd first thought. Her eyes, though rheumy and dull, were the eyes of a young woman. Her hands were equally youthful.

"What's your name?" Laszlo asked.

"I am Marie-France de Guiche," the woman said, a little proudly.

73

"How old are you?" Laszlo asked, not entirely certain if it was a proper question to ask of a strange woman.

"I'm not sure," Marie-France answered.

◆   ◆   ◆

When Rita and Kalman returned, the woman was fast asleep on the bed with Gizi curled up at her feet.

"Is that Muno?" Kalman asked anxiously.

"No," Laszlo whispered. "Sit down and I'll explain. I made soup."

They gathered around the table, Laszlo filled the bowls, then told them only what he had to about Marie-France: that she had escaped the priest's dungeon with Muno's help, that Muno had suggested she come to them for help. He didn't breathe a word about the messages Muno had sent, and hoped the woman wouldn't either.

Kalman was certain the hills would soon be filled with men with torches, guns, and dogs. Harboring Marie-France would be a serious offense. He wanted her out of the house as soon as possible.

"Oh, Kalman," Rita whispered. "No one's going out into the cold looking for that poor girl. She's barely alive."

They tiptoed over to the bed and watched her sleep.

"I suppose you're right," Kalman whispered.

When they'd finished supper and were sipping tea by the fire, Laszlo asked what had happened in the woods with the strange black wolf.

"He was alone and, by the looks of him, had been that way for weeks," Rita said. "He smelled of bugs and mice so he hadn't resorted to raiding farms yet, thank goodness. We took him to Fridrik."

She paused and her expression sank. "You could see he was mourning. He was as noble and steady as ever, but there was grief in his bark."

"Bertok — that's the name we've given the lone wolf — submitted immediately," Kalman said, "but Fridrik was wary. The process takes time. Bertok will have to prove himself before he's allowed in."

Laszlo was used to this sort of thing happening. Over the years his parents had been intimately involved in the lives of the wolf pack, warning them of hunters and poachers, alerting them to traps and sometimes helping them out of them, and occasionally negotiating with an errant wolf or rogue pack. The wolves more than returned the favors. More than once, a wolf had led a young, impetuous, and hopelessly lost Laszlo back home, or had showed up to steer him away from danger. And there was the time, when Laszlo was six and burning up with fever, that an uncharacteristically distraught Rita sent Kalman to seek the pack's help in finding some belladonna root. Laszlo could not ever remember a time when a smile had been so far from his mother's lips. Kalman found Agnes and she led him over several mountains to the base of a hill where a lone belladonna plant was tucked inside a fallen tree trunk. Kalman snatched it up and carried it home as fast as he could. Rita brewed the root into an elixir and spooned it into Laszlo's mouth. The next morning, his fever had broken.

"How long will it take?" Laszlo asked. He felt for Bertok. No one ought to be alone in the world.

Kalman shook his head. "As long as it takes," he said. "And in the end, Fridrik might send him away. Not every lone wolf is taken in." He looked over at Marie-France slumbering in the bed. "Perhaps we should adopt that policy."

"Oh, Kalman," Rita said. "What an awful thing to say."

Kalman sighed. "Yes," he said. "Forgive me. Fear gets the better of me sometimes."

Laszlo spent the next day looking over his shoulder. Marie-France did not waken in the morning, nor in the afternoon, and was still asleep as the sun began to set. There had been no unexpected visitors from town.

Rita cooked a soup with peas and the final cabbage of the year, and Kalman chipped at the last of the now petrified loaf. Before long he gave up on his knife and got out his hammer and a chisel.

As the soup stewed, the aroma of thyme and tarragon reached the nostrils of their sleeping houseguest. She rose up on her elbows, bleary-eyed and confused.

"Good night, Marie-France de Guiche," Rita chirped. "Just in time for supper."

◆　◆　◆

Marie-France convalesced for several days, sleeping and eating and walking about the farm. Each day added color to her cheeks. What had been lost slowly began to return. The family still knew practically nothing about her — how old she was, where she was from, where her family was, why she had been imprisoned — for she rarely spoke. She behaved much like a child: new to the world, leery of it yet it in awe of it, unaware of how much of herself she kept to herself. She contributed to the family by darning and knitting, and spent many hours in the fields with Laszlo, doing needlework.

The family soon forgot their fears of a search party.

"Apparently she's not worth the effort," Rita said one day.

"Then why did they keep her?" Laszlo asked.

"That's a question I would love to hear Père Raoul answer."

When Sunday came again, Rita surprised everyone by suggesting they attend mass. Naturally Kalman objected, but

Rita argued that it would be far less suspicious for them to go than not to. It was best to remain conspicuous, she said, conspicuous and devout. Laszlo remained quiet as they discussed it. He very much wanted to go to the village and had faith that Rita would prevail.

She did; they went to town. Of course, Marie-France remained behind with strict instructions from Kalman to stay out of sight should anyone appear.

There was no word in the village that day of an escaped prisoner, and, sadly for Laszlo, there was no sign of Muno. Once mass concluded the family milled about long enough to give the priest the impression that they genuinely wanted to be a part of things in Saint-Eustache, which in truth they did. When they returned home, they found Marie-France wrapped in a blanket, sound asleep under a tree near the sheepfold. Her mending was atop Kalman's volume of Virgil, which lay beside her.

"She reads," Kalman said approvingly.

Rita went off to the house to begin the evening meal. Kalman asked Laszlo to chop wood for the fire, then went off to tend to his cheese barrels. Laszlo lingered a minute, watching Marie-France sleep and trying to find the best way to phrase the question that he'd been wanting to ask her, when suddenly she opened her eyes. Seeing him standing over her made her start.

"It's only me," Laszlo said, crouching beside her. "I'm sorry if I startled you."

"I guess I dozed off," Marie-France said, regaining her composure. She sat up and smoothed her hair with her palm.

"I wanted to ask you something," Laszlo said uncertainly.

"Yes?"

"Muno said to tell me that our secret was safe."

The woman nodded.

"Did she tell you —" He swallowed hard, then tried again. "Did she tell you what the secret was?"

"No," Marie-France said. "There wasn't time."

Laszlo tried to hide his relief, but it showed on his face.

"I want to help her," he said. "I can't stand not knowing what is happening to her, and I don't really believe that she can escape anytime she wants."

"She got me out without any trouble," Marie-France said.

"I know, but —"

"You must leave her alone, Laszlo. She knows what she's doing. She's been living in the church a long time. She knows how things operate there. It was she who fed me, you know. If she hadn't, I would have died. She sneaked me food at the risk of her own life because she knew that they had forgotten about me. Then, when she was imprisoned, she was somehow able to free herself and come to me. Believe me, she knows —"

"— what she's doing, yes, I know," Laszlo said. "But what if she waits too long to act? What if they come for her and . . ."

"I suppose that's possible. I always waited for someone to come for me. After a while, I hoped they would." She looked away. "But I'm glad they didn't."

"But they could for her," Laszlo said.

"She would know. Don't ask me how, but she would, and she'd escape."

"But we can't just let her rot in there."

Marie-France's eyes shifted downward. "No, no one should rot in there."

"No," Laszlo said, realizing what she meant. He reached over and touched her hand.

"Is that from dyeing wool?" she asked, looking at the patch of vivid red skin that nearly covered the back of his hand.

"No," he said. "It's a birthmark. My mother calls it a strawberry. She says when she first saw it, she knew I'd survive." He looked down. "Two of my brothers died before I was born. They were just babies. My mother says the strawberry is where God kissed me."

Marie-France looked up at him, a sad smile on her face.

"I'm ready to leave now," she said.

"Leave?" Laszlo said.

"Yes. I was only passing through Saint-Eustache when I was arrested. I was on my way to my uncle's house." She paused and her eyes moistened. "I did nothing wrong, you know. A merchant accused me of stealing, but all I'd done was resist his touch. He touched me in a way . . . well, in a way I did not like him to. Père Raoul called me terrible names in court — a wastrel, a thief, even a witch. He said I had cast a spell on the man. It was preposterous. I was not allowed to speak. No witnesses were called except the man who accused me. They wouldn't allow me to send word to my uncle. I was thrown into the dungeon and shackled to the wall. This was years ago, I'm sure, though I have no idea how many."

Laszlo set his hand on her shoulder. She blinked and tears streamed down her cheeks.

"Now I want to continue on my way. My uncle must have worried terribly. I imagine by now he has given me up for dead. Even so, I want to go to him. I want to put all this behind me."

"I don't know if you're strong enough," Laszlo said.

"It's not far. I'll go slowly and rest often."

"If you'll let me," Laszlo said, "I'll take you in the cart."

◆　◆　◆

Kalman said no, then yes, then no again, then yes again. His final reasoning was this: as risky as the trip seemed, the family would rest more easily without Marie-France under their roof. He did insist that he go along, however, and that they travel after dark. The moon would be bright enough to light their way. He knew the village where her uncle lived, or, at least *had* lived when Marie-France was arrested. It was two days' walk if they followed Kalman's less traveled, more circuitous route through the woods.

Rita wanted to go along, too. Kalman protested. Someone, he said, should look after the farm. Rita persisted. Kalman refused. Then Rita whispered something in his ear and, as if by magic, Kalman gave in. Laszlo could not imagine what she had said.

Gizi was left behind to watch over the flock and, as an added safety measure, Kalman disobeyed his own moratorium and went into the woods as a wolf to let the pack know they would be away. Fridrik and Agnes gave their assurance that they would look in on the farm periodically until the family returned.

They set out after supper, Rita, Kalman, and Laszlo taking turns pulling the two-wheeled wooden cart while Marie-France slept inside. The two of them who didn't pull pushed. They crossed the meadows then stepped inside the forest, leaving most of the moonlight behind them. Laszlo supposed that if he were a boy in some other family he might have felt afraid then, but he knew there wasn't anything to fear. Most forest animals, he knew, stayed well clear of human beings. Even the larger ones, like bears, didn't pose much of a threat. And of course the wolves were nothing to worry about.

The path through the woods wound up and down and around so much Laszlo thought that at any minute they would be out on the meadow again. After a while of this, the hour drew past the family's usual bedtime and Laszlo began to tire behind the cart. Rita told Kalman to stop, then persuaded Laszlo to climb in beside Marie-France.

He awoke in the morning to a linnet's song. Dew had formed on his face and clothes. He sat up and saw the dawn streaming in horizontally through the trees.

"Good morning," Rita said to him. She was already up and stoking a campfire. "Tea will be ready soon. Want to collect more wood for me?"

After breakfast they packed up and started off again. Marie-France, who had risen at the smell of porridge, walked awhile in the beginning, but then, exhausted, had to be put back into the cart. The trek that second day was more strenuous than it had been the first, as it was mostly uphill. By midday they had reached the top of a high peak. At their feet lay the sprawling green mountains of the great Pyrenees range. A sense of relief washed over Laszlo, not only because they had finished their climb, but also because they were completely surrounded by benign living things. Being so removed from the human world was comforting to him, though the comfort of that remove carried with it a measure of sorrow. It did not please him to be so glad to be rid of people.

From that peak they traveled along a saddle to another, and then along another saddle to a third one. At least, Laszlo thought, they were going up and down rather than up and up. From the third peak, Laszlo saw the top of a large granite cirque breaking through the tree line below. The formation of rock was so precisely circular that it seemed to Laszlo it couldn't possibly have evolved on its own, that it had to have been carved by human hands. But then he thought of the perfect circles of the moon, of the ripples of raindrops on water, of the eye, and he changed his mind.

From there they descended back into the forest. Then at last, just after sundown, they emerged onto a wide open meadow high above a river valley, in which was tucked a small, fortified village.

"That's it," Kalman said. "Montcorbeau."

Marie-France sat up immediately. A little smile lit on her lips as she gazed down on the sleeping village.

"Montcorbeau," she said softly.

To everyone's surprise, she leapt down from the cart and flung her arms around Rita.

84

"Oh, thank you!" she wept. "Thank you, thank you, thank you!"

She also hugged a nonplussed Kalman, and then Laszlo. Her happiness radiated into him.

"Wouldn't you like us to come to your uncle's with you, to be sure he's still there?" Rita asked.

"Now, Rita," Kalman said sternly, "we talked about this and decided we would come this far and no farther."

"*You* decided, you mean," Rita said.

"It could be dangerous."

"It could be more dangerous for her."

"He's still there," Marie-France interrupted. "I'm sure of it."

Rita shot her a skeptical look. "I'm not going anywhere until you find your uncle and let us know you're all right."

Kalman clucked his tongue, but said nothing.

Marie-France hugged Rita again. "I will never forget your kindness," she said into her ear.

She squeezed Laszlo again. "You have given me my life back, Laszlo!" she said. Then she danced away down the hill in the moonlight.

Laszlo waved and waved, but she did not look back. He hoped for her sake that Montcorbeau was different from Saint-Eustache, that it had no dungeon or pillories or burnings. Kalman would have said that all of the villages in

Europe had them, but Laszlo preferred to believe that this one was different. He chose to believe that Marie-France would never be unhappy again, that the rest of her life would be filled with laughter and dancing and singing, for she had done a life's share of suffering already.

An hour later Marie-France reappeared at the village gates, jumping up and down and waving her arms. A man stood beside her, waving his.

"He's there!" Laszlo said.

"Thank heaven," Rita laughed.

"Good," Kalman said. "Let's go."

CHAPTER SEVEN

They slept in the woods again that night. In the morning, they faced the steep slope they had descended the night before.

"I wouldn't be surprised if we found Noah's ark sitting up at the top of this mountain," Rita said to Laszlo as they pushed the cart upward. "I ask you, what sort of god drowns an entire world of people and animals? If they disappointed Him, whose fault was that?"

Laszlo, too, had always been perplexed by the story of the ark, though for a different reason. What he could never settle in his mind was whether two werewolves had been invited aboard.

They didn't reach the summit until well after noon. Rita sank onto the ground.

"I don't know about the men in this family," she said, "but I'm a bit weary."

Laszlo and Kalman collapsed on either side of her.

"We can't rest long," Kalman said, panting between his words.

Rita hissed at him.

When they were moving once more along the crest, saddle to peak, saddle to peak, the cirque came back into view. Laszlo began to call his mother's attention to it when, quite unexpectedly, Kalman steered the cart off the path. Laszlo glanced over at his mother and saw that she was grinning.

"What's he doing?" he asked.

She didn't answer.

Kalman wheeled the cart behind a brushwood, then reappeared without it. From the path, the cart could not be seen.

"Why are we stopping here?" Laszlo asked. "What's going on?"

Kalman and Rita both smiled.

"What is it?" Laszlo said in a demanding voice. He was beginning to feel anxious, and it was making him cross.

"It's time, Laszlo," Rita said.

Laszlo squinted at her, and she and Kalman both nodded. He remembered how his mother had whispered something in Kalman's ear that had persuaded him to come.

could see their eyes gleaming at the other end of the crevice. He pressed his head in and, to his relief, it fit, though only just. His shoulders proved more of a challenge. He wished he'd thought to shed his clothes as his parents had. And he wished like mad that he could become a wolf like them, that he could be sleek and limber, which he would be, *if only he could squeeze through the wall!* He pushed with all his might and didn't budge even the slightest bit.

"I can't make it!" he grunted.

His parents didn't seem to be concerned, which had the effect of emboldening him. If they weren't worried, he thought, why should he be? He peered ahead into the gap and saw his mother's snout poking into it. She began to howl very low and the sound of it was oddly familiar to Laszlo. And then he knew: it was her old song from Erdély.

Laszlo closed his eyes and tried not to think about where he was. He tried not to think about *what* he was. He was not a boy stuck in a rock wall. He was the wind. He was water in a stream. His body loosened some at the joints and he inched forward. His cloak — his *new* cloak — snagged on a rock and tore. Laszlo didn't care. He released his breath and pressed forward. The tear in his cloak widened. His clogs slipped off. When he inhaled, the wall closed back in around him. He was sure he had wedged himself in for good. A wave of panic swept over him, but he kept his head enough to remember to exhale and soon his mother's song was seeping back into his ears. As the last bit of air escaped his lips he slid forward, out of his cloak. He tightened his diaphragm to keep air from re-entering, then wriggled still forward. The rough surface of the rock scraped at his bare skin. His head poked out the other side, then his shoulders, and then he poured out of the crevice onto the ground, naked as the day he was born.

The first thing he felt was his mother's cold nose on his warm belly, then his father's. They frolicked around him like pups, nudging him and pawing at him.

"Easy!" he said. "You're scratching me!"

They backed off and he climbed to his feet. Around him were the white-barked birch trees he'd seen through the chinks. His parents ran around him, grazing his cold, bare flesh with their fur, then they suddenly turned and darted off into the brush.

"Wait!" Laszlo called, running after them.

They moved with astonishing speed through the undergrowth. Laszlo, without a heavy fur coat, without paws, pads, and claws, had a much harder time. Thin, bloody streaks crisscrossed his bare limbs and torso.

"Wait!" he called again. "I can't keep up!"

He ran deeper into the brush, growing more savage the farther he went, until in time he came to bear almost no resemblance at all to the kindly shepherd boy who so often sat knitting under a tree, and bore more resemblance to a feral creature of the woods.

From time to time his parents returned, circling playfully around him, nudging him onward, then tearing off again. The encouragement worked. He kept on until he had ripped himself free of the forest and stepped out into a clearing. The canopy of the forest reached over it, casting it in mottled shadows. In the center of the clearing was a small mountain pool, its water clear and still. There were no grasses or reeds at its edges, no algae or water lilies floating upon it.

Burning with thirst, Laszlo rushed to the pool's edge, but when he knelt to drink, the sight of the pool's surface made him gasp. The day was bright and sunny and the water was as still as a pane of glass, yet neither the sun nor the branches overhead were mirrored in it. Laszlo leaned out and looked down. No image of himself looked back. He leaned in closer. Not a shadow, not an outline of his head, appeared on the surface.

"It's a wolving pool," said his father from behind him.

Laszlo was so startled that he nearly toppled in. He spun around to find his parents standing behind him, human again.

As he looked at them, his mind nearly numb with anticipation, he saw them in a way he never had before. He realized he resembled them more than they resembled each other. Those sloping shoulders of Kalman's, those slender fingers of Rita's, Kalman's knobby knees, the dark circles around Rita's eyes, Kalman's wavy hair and wild eyebrows: put them all together and you got Laszlo Emberek.

Laszlo had watched many lambs come into the world and he had never had any trouble identifying the parentage of any of them. Henriette, for example, was lamb to Babette, Pernette to Henriette, and of course Alphonse was father to both. It had been so with all the dozens of sheep he'd known and loved over the years. But he had never put himself to the test, he had never thought of himself as having been *bred* as much as he did right at that minute.

Rita stepped toward him and set her hands on his shoulders.

"You don't have to, you know," she said. "It's your decision."

It was a decision Laszlo had spent his life thinking about. Sometimes it seemed as if he never thought of anything else. He'd known for a long time that he'd have a choice when his time came. His parents had told him so years before, and often reminded him of it, in order that he could take his time deciding what to do. And he had decided. He understood, or thought he did, what changing meant. He knew he would have to live as his parents had al-

93

ways lived: cautiously, judiciously, invisibly. He knew what would happen if his nature was ever discovered. Despite that, he'd never dreamed of becoming anything other than what his parents were. How could he not leap at the chance to find out how it felt to be in the skin of another creature?

"I want to change," he said.

Rita smiled. "Then dive in. Swim to the other shore. Don't come up until you reach it."

"We'll be there when you do," Kalman said.

Laszlo turned back to face the pool. Considering the season, he assumed the water would be freezing. He stepped up to the edge. To his astonishment, a reflection of a wolf looked up at him. It was silver-haired with flecks of white fur running down its throat and bushy dark tufts over its brown eyes.

Its eyes were his eyes.

He dipped a toe into the pool. It did not cause a ripple. He pulled it back out; there was no splash, no sound. Perplexed, he picked up a pebble and tossed it in. The pebble was swallowed up without a trace. He tossed in a small stick and the pool absorbed it, too, without the slightest disturbance.

"Look!" he said, whirling around, but his parents were gone.

"Mama?" he called out. "Papa?"

The only answer was howling. Laszlo took a deep breath, closed his eyes, and dove in.

The water wasn't cold. On the contrary, it was warmer than fresh sheep's milk. The warmth of it spread through his torso, out his limbs to his fingers and toes, up his neck to his face and ears. It was unlike the warmth he felt sitting under the summer sun, or drinking tea by the fire in winter, or being held by his mother. The heat penetrated his bones, melted his fears, soothed his mind. Though he was completely submerged in water, Laszlo felt like a flame licking from the wick of a candle, like the sun itself.

He opened his eyes and saw the opposite bank ahead. The force of his dive had propelled him halfway there. He easily paddled the rest of the way without need of a breath, then broke through the surface without a ripple. As he grappled for something at the water's edge with which to pull himself out, he was astonished to find that he did so not with a hand, but with a *paw*. The fur was silver except for a patch of deep red, which looked as if it had been dyed with madder root: his birthmark. Heavy black claws poked out of the fur of his toes.

Instinctively he kicked with his hind legs and scrambled easily, and splashlessly, out of the pool. Water didn't drip from his coat; his fur wasn't even damp. He ducked his head between his forelegs and saw a furry brisket and silvery hind legs and, swishing back and forth behind them, a bushy tail! He spun around to see what he looked like in the water's surface, but there, staring back at him, was the reflection of a boy with dark wavy hair and wild eyebrows.

A wolf howled then and Laszlo raised his head high, and that was when he learned that it was not only he that had changed. The world had. He no longer stood in a softly fragrant forest with the gentle twitterings of birds and insects providing a backdrop. It was now a place noisier and smellier than the village square. The odors were so strong that it was as if Laszlo were seeing them rather than smelling them. Amazingly, Laszlo knew exactly where the smells came from and what was producing them. There, in those ferns, for example, were day-old capercaillie droppings; in that shrub, a rotting beetle being picked at by a marmot; over that ridge, a freshly fallen birch already infested with termites. Wolf markings were everywhere. Laszlo surmised that they were made by hundreds if not thousands — or more? — of new werewolves, like him. Without giving it a second thought, he lifted a leg and mingled his scent with the others.

As for the noise, the cry of a raven overhead was as piercing as if the bird were perched on his shoulder. He heard not only the sweet chirruping of a coal tit but also the scritching of its talons on its roost. A mouse gnawing a seed crunched louder than Laszlo's flock did diving into a mangerful of grain. When he heard the paddling of two wolves' paws on dried leaves, he could tell how fast the animals were moving and which (the one in front) was larger. He knew by their scents that they were mates, and even what their last meal had been: sheep cheese.

"Papa! Mama!" Laszlo howled, and that was exactly how it came out — a howl.

He caught them out of the corner of his eye as they flickered through the trees in silvery flashes and realized that his sense of sight, which he'd almost forgotten he possessed, seemed sharper out the corners of his eyes. His parents reached the clearing, pranced up to him, their heads and tails high, Kalman's a bit higher. Laszlo dropped his head so that a smooth line curved from his nose to the tip of his tail. He whimpered and pawed at the ground. Rita let out a yawp and then she and Kalman sprinted away again into the woods. Laszlo, elated at the prospect of trying out his new legs, sprinted after them.

He ran with such speed that it at first frightened him. His stride was swift and compact, his body, narrow; his legs, long and thin, had a deceptively relaxed gait about them, but were strong and graceful; his hind paws landed in the exact same spot his forepaws had, eliminating wasted energy, streamlining his forward motion. Ducking branches and clearing logs was much simpler without elbows and clothing to snag, with claws instead of clogs. It was like being back in the pool: he swam through the woods.

New smells swirled around him but he held them at bay, staying locked on his parents' scents, following them as he would a path. Rita and Kalman did not slow down for him but continued at full gallop around and around within the circle of stones, goading Laszlo into finding his legs. He did not need to be goaded; nothing on earth could have stopped him from taking full advantage of his newfound abilities, from exploiting every muscle, every ounce of speed. Nothing, that is, save a low-hanging branch. It hooked him under the chin and flipped him onto his back.

His parents reappeared and fell upon him, pawing and licking and nipping at him like pups. They bared their fangs and snarled, but it was all in fun. Laszlo nipped and snarled back, but eventually had to submit; they were too much for him. They then tore off again with Laszlo in happy pursuit. This time they let him keep apace as they sped once more around the pool, then slipped back out through the crack in the wall. To Laszlo's great joy and relief, this time he passed through it like thread through a needle's eye.

When he emerged, however, he was disappointed to find that Rita and Kalman had resumed their human form.

"We need to get back, son," Kalman said.

"So says your father," Rita said, rolling her eyes. "But don't worry, Laszlo. This isn't the last time. It's the first."

Laszlo whined a little, but when he saw it was no use, he turned around, fished his torn clothes out of the crevice with his teeth, then . . .

How was he supposed to change back?

Neither Kalman nor Rita had said a word about it and, in the state he was in, he couldn't very well ask. Did he have to go back through the pool? His parents never had to. They changed back and forth at will, whenever and wherever they wanted. But how? Why hadn't they told him? He looked up at them, his head low, and whimpered. They paid him no mind. Clearly he was going to have to figure it out for himself.

However it was done, he decided, it must be done within, by some thought, some wish. He was going to have to *will* it to happen. It was then, as he stood there thinking, that it dawned on him that he was still himself, that his thoughts and feelings, even his memories, were still his own. He was some sort of blend of boy and wolf. The wolf part of his mind read what his nose "saw"; the human part put it into words. When he changed back, would his mind change, too, or would the wolf part remain? Would he be different now, no matter what form his body took? Had he changed for good?

With all of this going on in his head, he began to feel more human, even with the fur and the snout and the tail. Without his realizing it, his human mind — his human words, his human fears — were drowning out his wolf senses. The smells of the forest no longer overwhelmed him. The raven no longer deafened him. He suddenly felt vulnerable there in the woods, a wolfling without his senses, without his family, without his pack. He wanted to be a boy again.

And then he was: a boy on his hands and knees on the ground.

Rita helped him to his feet. "Isn't it wonderful?" she said, wrapping him in her arms.

Laszlo soaked in the warmth of her body, let her force out the chill that had seeped back into him since losing his fur.

"It's a gift," she breathed in his ear. "Don't ever believe anyone who tells you otherwise."

CHAPTER EIGHT

When the family returned home the next day, they found themselves with plenty to do. There were repairs to Alphonse's pen to be made, wool dyes to be prepared, yarn to be spun, and the enormous task of collecting and bundling the hay and straw for the winter fodder. But, as always, tending to the sheep remained top priority.

When Laszlo entered the fold, Claudette, Henriette, and Pernette huddled together, bleating in loud, flat tones.

"I'm still me," Laszlo said to them, though he couldn't say it with complete confidence. He wasn't a different person than the one he'd been when they'd left for Montcorbeau, but then again, he wasn't exactly the same either.

As he'd suspected, the wolf did not disappear when he reverted to human form, just as the human did not disappear when he'd been a wolf. The boy and the wolf were now knit together, like two skeins of yarn into one fabric. Laszlo's senses were not as acute as when he'd been a wolf, but they were keener than they had ever been before. As many times as he'd been in the sheepfold, never had he been so besot by its smells. To his chagrin, he could almost *taste* it.

Only Babette, who had known him the longest, was brave enough to allow him to come near. She did not flinch when he set his palm against her neck, or crouched beside her. When she looked in his eyes, her fear was completely assuaged. The others followed the cue of their elder and inched warily forward. After all, it was not unusual for the flock to have a wolf in their midst. Laszlo stared into each one's eyes and the transition was made.

He and Gizi then led them out to pasture. Gizi never batted an eye at his master's new constitution. If anything, she was warmer toward him than ever. Laszlo decided this was because they were more alike now: they each had wolf in them.

It was the wolf in Laszlo that let him know that Fridrik was on his way toward the flushing before the wolf appeared in the cornflowers. Laszlo raised his horn and blew. To his surprise, Fridrik responded with a long, deep howl. In all the times Laszlo had encountered wolves in the fields, none had ever howled when he'd blown the horn. He paced nervously as he waited for his mother or father to appear. Hopefully they would know what the howl meant. He waited a long time, so long that he began to worry that something was wrong, that maybe that was the reason Fridrik had come: to send him home. He blew the horn again, louder. Fridrik howled again, louder. Again Laszlo waited; again no one came.

And then, as if struck by lightning, Laszlo understood.

"Oh!" he said. "He's calling *me!*"

He set his horn down in the grass, pulled his cloak over his head, then, his palms out, fell forward. As he fell, he thought about how much he wanted to go with Fridrik, side by side with him as a wolf, and when he landed, he did so on four paws. Fridrik turned and loped back across the field toward the woods, and Laszlo eagerly ran after him.

◆　◆　◆

The second that Laszlo set foot inside the forest he was descended on by a pack of wolves. Fortunately, they were all friends. Agnes was among them, and her sister, Aunt Rozsa, who had three legs (she'd lost the fourth to a trap years before), and last spring's pups, now grown into their large paws. Laszlo had never laid eyes on the pups before but had heard all about them from his parents. There were two males, whom his parents called Daniel and Zoltan, and a female, Klotild. Kalman believed that Zoltan, the strongest and fiercest of the trio, would be Fridrik's likely successor, but Rita was partial to Daniel, who she called a true diplomat. In truth, Rita's favorite was Klotild, who she thought would one day succeed Agnes. Rita called her both strong *and* diplomatic.

One by one the wolves approached Laszlo, tails raised to a height reflecting their status. As the visitor, Laszlo kept his low. The whole procedure was quite ceremonial, and Laszlo was delighted at how naturally he played his part in it. Only one of the pups, a male, growled at him, and Laszlo surmised that he was Zoltan. Apparently, lowering his tail was not adequately submissive, so Laszlo rolled over on his back and exposed his belly. Zoltan lunged, his fangs bared, but at the last moment Klotild edged her way in and bumped him out of the way. She set her opened jaws over Laszlo's throat and the scent of recently eaten rat saturated his nostrils. He whimpered as pitiably as he could, causing Klotild to leap away and race around him in a wide circle. Zoltan chased after her, snarling and nipping at her tail, no doubt angry at her for acting above what he believed was her station. The third pup, Daniel, penetrated their circle, trotted up to Laszlo, and licked him on the snout. Laszlo took this as an invitation to play, which he wholeheartedly accepted.

The games the young wolves played changed quickly

and often. They played at being allies in a hunt, at being enemies, at being clumsy newborn pups rolling around on the ground. Then they tore off through the forest at top speed, their strong hearts racing, their long legs pumping. Laszlo got walloped by branches several times, but always jumped right back into the fray. He was, however, too new to wolving to be able to keep up with his new friends. At last he gave up and collapsed into a pile of rotting leaves. Daniel came over, his head high, and stared down into Laszlo's eyes. Daniel was a black wolf, like the others, but had more sprinklings of gray in his coat, as if he'd been lightly dusted with ash. What was especially striking about him, though, were his eyes. It wasn't their shape or color. They all had the same amber-colored eyes. There was something — a light of some kind — in Daniel's that made Laszlo trust him.

As he thought about Daniel, Laszlo began to wonder what the pack had been thinking of him. What sort of wolf did they judge him to be? Was he awkward and naive like a new pup? Did he project brashness like Zoltan, or cunning like Klotild, or confidence like Daniel? What did they see in his eyes? He knew it would take time for him to find out. Like any new wolf, he would have to await acceptance from the leaders.

Laszlo had heard over and over from his parents how wrong people's perceptions were about wolves, how they were not the bloodthirsty man-eaters they were believed to be. In his afternoon with the pack Laszlo had seen for himself what they were like. Most prominently, the wolves behaved as a family, much like Laszlo's own. They toiled and played and ate together, and they squabbled, too, but there was never any question of the tenderness they felt for one another. Fridrik and Agnes dealt patiently and fairly with the pups, only interceding when the play got too rough, and then gently, with the nudging of noses. And the pups, for all of their shows of aggression, were the best of friends. What Laszlo found most surprising, and enchanting, was how doting they could be to one another. Being with the wolves made Laszlo proud to be, in some way, their kin.

Finally, remembering that he had duties to fulfill back on the flushing, Laszlo bid the pack farewell. As he was leaving, he scented the arrival of a new wolf. It was Bertok, the lone wolf that had come to the farm, the one his parents had led to Fridrik, the one who was waiting for admittance to the pack. Laszlo then saw his yellow eyes peering out from behind a copse of birch trees. Bertok was black, too, though his paws were gray, like old socks. His dejection was apparent on his face and in his posture. Laszlo glanced back at Fridrik and Agnes, their snouts pointing slightly up, ears pointing heavenward, and hoped that they would be merciful.

Rita and Kalman refused Laszlo's pleas to attend mass with him again that Sunday, saying they simply had too much to do. Rita did argue, though, that Laszlo ought to be allowed to go alone. "I can take my spinning out on the flushing with the flock," she said. "I think it would be wise to remain in the priest's good graces."

As always, Kalman objected and objected, then relented.

The trip to town was unlike any Laszlo had ever made. For one thing, aside from birds and bugs, he saw no animals. This was peculiar; usually, at the very least, he saw squirrels and rabbits. But even stranger was the fact that, though he saw none, he knew without a doubt that the forest was virtually teeming with wildlife. It had been years since Laszlo had seen a bear in the woods, yet he smelled — but didn't see — *two* of them that morning. He also smelled a small herd of ibex not far away, and even heard the pounding of their hoofbeats. The prospect of tracking them down was tempting, but tracking bear and ibex would have made him late for mass.

Farther on, as Laszlo neared a more pungent than usual swine farm, he saw a herd of pigs gathered at the base of an oak tree, gorging on the acorns that the swineherd shook free from a branch above. The pigs squealed very loudly as

Laszlo passed by, louder than they ever had before, and Laszlo felt he knew why. The swineherd glared down at him from the tree, but Laszlo just waved his customary hearty hello.

"Good morning, Laszlo," Egmont said when Laszlo reached the village gate. "Got your Bible, I see. Well, mustn't be late for mass." He pulled open the huge door.

"I think I'm early," Laszlo said as he stepped inside.

"Well then there's time for quoits," Egmont said.

Laszlo just nodded. He had never been invited to join in the village boys' games. "I don't think so," he said. "Good-bye, Egmont."

"See you afterward, my boy," Egmont said.

Laszlo sat down under a shade tree, pulled out his drop spindle and a hank of wool, and began spinning it into yarn. Being the sabbath, the shops and smithies were all shuttered. No grain was milled, no horses shod, no teeth pulled. The pious men of the community — the curates, the members of the Fabric, though not Père Raoul — sat on benches in the parish garden, their hands folded in silent meditation. The rest of the men of the village rolled dice in shadowy corners or spoke boisterously together in groups about hunting, taxes, their wives, their livestock, the harvest, and people not present. The women sat in their own groups doing needlework and talking only a tad less noisily.

The young girls moved together in flocks, touching one another freely, bleating often, and skittering from one place to another — like young ewes, Laszlo thought. The young rams did much the same, only their touch was rougher, with elbows and fists instead of fingers and palms. Each group pretended to be ignorant of the other, but it was no secret that glances were constantly being made back and forth. One of the games the boys played had them divided into two teams and kicking around a sewn leather ball. It seemed to Laszlo merely an excuse for the rams to show the ewes how tough they could be. The boys were muddy, sweaty, scraped, and bruised, and clearly quite happy about it. Laszlo thought it looked like fun, but, of course, no one had invited him to play. He told himself he didn't mind.

When the bells chimed for mass, Laszlo put his spinning away and darted for the church doors, provoking more than one person to comment on the strangeness of a boy running toward church rather than away from it. Once everyone was inside and seated, the seigneur and his wife made their entrance. Madame Pussort wore a sparkling silver necklace bedecked with red and green gems. She looked up or down or at her husband, but never out at the room of dirty, smelly herdsmen, peddlers, gravediggers, and the like. The seigneur, however, sat with his shoulders straight and his gaze steadily trained on his subjects, the peasants who worked like mules every day (except Sunday) to scrape up the money to pay his levies in order that he could afford to buy his wife glittering jewels. He dared them to find him anything less than the finest gentleman they had ever seen, and none in attendance met his challenge. Hate him they did, but envy him they did also. There was silence in the church as the congregation stared up at the lordly couple, silence, that is, except for coughing and spitting and the growling of stomachs.

Then from behind the crowd Père Raoul stepped into the church, waving his censer. Laszlo could see only his biretta bobbing above the heads of the churchgoers, so he elbowed his way through the crowd to the aisle. As Père Raoul passed, a trail of smoke and incense behind him, Laszlo spied Muno in the haze, adorned in her drab woolen tunic with the yellow cross sewn onto it. His relief turned quickly to concern, though, as he realized how changed she was. The skin of her face seemed stretched even more tightly than before. Her eye sockets were sunken, the whites of her eyes, gray and lifeless. She staggered after the priest, awkward as a new lamb.

When they reached the front of the hall, Père Raoul solemnly acknowledged the presence of the seigneuriàl couple, then addressed the congregation in Latin. Laszlo didn't listen to a word of the mass, being too intent on training his senses on the frail-looking young girl kneeling on the wooden floor behind the priest. Laszlo's nose told him that she had not eaten that day, or the day before.

The service concluded with the monitory proclamation, in which Père Raoul read out, in French, a list of crimes recently committed against God and his children. The crimes ran the gamut from drunkenness to thievery to heresy, and the congregation was assured that the guilty were either being punished soundly or soon would be.

"Any information helpful in ascertaining the identities of these wrongdoers will be greatly appreciated," the priest said, "and will set the informant firmly on the path to Paradise."

Then, hours after it had begun, the service ended.

The tavern door opened with the church's, and the worshipers dove headlong into goblets of wine and ale. A table filled with food, prepared and donated by the good people of the town, stretched across the churchyard. Père Raoul chatted with Seigneur Pussort (Madame had disappeared), the members of the Fabric, and several prominent merchants of the town. Muno remained at Père Raoul's heel.

As Laszlo was edging closer to them, trying to catch Muno's eye, a hand grasped him by the shoulder and spun him around. His eyes met those of a muddy-faced boy of about his own age. One of the boy's eyes was purple and swollen shut. His front teeth had either rotted away or had been knocked out.

"We need one more man," the boy huffed, then he grabbed Laszlo's arm and began dragging him away. Laszlo thought to tell the boy that he was mistaken — that he wasn't a man — but stopped himself. Maybe he was. After all, he'd been through the pool. He allowed himself to be led into the ruckus.

Once out on the playing field, which was merely a small, fenced-in area with thick, black mud, the boy thrust Laszlo into the midst of the ballplayers he'd seen brawling earlier. When he was assigned a side, both his opponents and his teammates sneered at him. The ball was then dropped into the center and the boys all roared and rushed at one another. Laszlo had no idea what the rules or the object of the game were, nor did he know any of the boys, which made distinguishing between friend and foe impossible. In the end, none of this seemed to matter. The real goal was for each boy to do as much bodily harm to as many of the other boys as possible, hopefully in full view of the girls across the yard.

Laszlo wasn't in the imbroglio ten seconds before a forearm caught him across the jaw, causing him to bite down hard on his tongue. He cried out in pain, reeled backward, and was instantly struck in the ribs by an elbow. He fell to his knees and was beaten into the mud by a stampede of bare feet. Two boys locked in combat then crashed down on top of him, one of their heads striking Laszlo's, the other's knee driving painfully into his thigh. Laszlo sprang up in a fury onto his hands and feet, his back arched, his limbs stiff. A vicious snarl burned in his throat.

The brutality ceased. The boys closest to Laszlo scrambled away, their eyes wild with alarm. Even some of the nearby adults stopped what they were doing and craned their necks to see what was happening.

The sudden silence transformed Laszlo's rage into raw panic. The stares were worse than the blows. What had happened? Had he *changed*? Could he have turned into a wolf right in front of everyone? He glanced down at his hands and sighed in relief that he still had fingers and thumbs. But, he wondered, had he changed and changed back already? He searched his mind: had he, even for a second, wished that he were a wolf?

"Did you hear that?" one of the boys said out of the side of his mouth.

Murmurs followed, growing in volume as they swept through the crowd. After a lifetime of no one ever looking Laszlo in the eye, the sight of them all staring at him at the same time was too much. He got up from his knees and took a few small steps backward. The crowd crept forward. Some of the boys jeered. Laszlo spun on his heel to run, but the crowd had moved in behind him. He dove into them, fighting his way through, slashing at them with his arms, his fists clenched. His ferocity surprised them — and him — and he worried again that he might change. At last he broke free and ran away into the maze of the village's narrow streets. Some of the boys ran after him, but Laszlo, his body energized by fear, was far too fast for them. One by one they gave up.

Then, as he dashed for Egmont and the gate, Laszlo spied something out of the corner of his eye. He stopped, and as he was gasping for breath, a familiar scent filled his nostrils. It was Muno. He caught a glimpse of her then, peering out at him from behind a wagon. She'd slipped away from the priest again. Laszlo couldn't imagine what possessed her to be so reckless.

He called her name and she took off in the opposite direction. He chased after her, weaving around wagons and carts and then down a dark alley strewn with bones and animal droppings. She stumbled and fell into the mud.

"Leave me alone!" she hissed when he caught up to her. "Just talking to you could mean the dungeon again!"

"Why aren't you with Père Raoul, then?" Laszlo said. "Why were you following me?"

"That's none of your concern," she said sharply. "I want you to stay away from me. Stay away from the church. I can't be seen with you!"

She climbed to her feet and started off down the alley

again, bracing herself against the wall with her hand. She clearly didn't have much strength.

"But I want to help you," Laszlo said.

"I don't need your help!" the girl snapped. "I don't *want* it. Leave me alone!"

Many emotions swept over Laszlo then: shock, shame, fear, guilt. He couldn't begin to sort them out. He did understand what an enormous error in judgment he'd made in going to town that day. Muno's message, relayed by Marie-France, had been explicit — *Stay away!* — yet he had brazenly defied it. Because of that, she now shunned him. Worse, the whole village was after him. The whispers had become an outcry.

Why had he done it? Standing there in that dark, reeking alleyway, the reasons became clear to him. He'd come to town to rescue her because he needed her. She was the only one who knew him for what he'd been before the wolving pool, who might have understood what it had done to him, what it meant to him. She was the only person he'd ever known who might have accepted him for what he was. He'd come for her because he needed a friend. Instead, he'd driven her away.

Once she disappeared around a corner, he returned down the alley, back out into the light, and was met by the sound of whispers pouring into his ears from all around. People peeked out of windows and doorways and around corners. They pointed at him. Some boys ran out into the open, down on all fours, pretending to be wild beasts, snarling and clawing at one another. A few more joined in, and then, from the shadows, the black figure of the priest appeared, his face stony, his eyes sharp as shearing blades.

Laszlo turned and ran in the direction of the gate, feeling like a hare pursued by a hunting party. A wish to become faster led to a wish to become a wolf, which he quickly put out of his mind.

When he reached the gate, he was relieved to find Egmont alone.

"What's the rush there, Laszlo?" Egmont said with a grin. "Ah, I know! Church is out!"

He swung the gate open, and Laszlo ran through it and away from the village as fast as he could.

kind. Their judgments couldn't penetrate his silver coat, his canine heart. If they knew what he was, he thought, what it was really like to be inside his skin, they would never persecute him. They would envy him.

The ibex herd sensed his coming and stampeded down from their rocky perch out onto open pasture. They moved together in formation as they ran across the meadow like a school of fish in a stream. They were fast, but to Laszlo's delight, he was faster. With a burst of speed, he headed them off — as he had seen Gizi do to the flock so many times — and was actually able to change their course, bend their will. The power was exhilarating. This was nothing like leading domesticated sheep. These were wild goats, ornery and dangerous, with razor-sharp hooves and horns like scimitars poised to hurl an unwary wolf head over tail, or perhaps even run it through. But the wolf and the shepherd sides of Laszlo merged into one proficient ibexherd, keen to the animals' feints and gambits. He drove them around the open meadows, growling and snarling and nipping at their flanks when they didn't obey, keeping them away from the woods where he knew they'd scatter. He wasn't sure how he knew these things, only that he did. The dread he'd felt in town was a thing of the past. He'd escaped into another world.

And then came a blast. The hide of the lead ibex — a big,

sturdy male — burst open, spraying the herd, and Laszlo, with its blood. It fell and was trampled into the ground by the herd. The scents hit Laszlo's nose then, one after the other: gunpowder, dogs, people. He had been so absorbed in his herding that he had somehow filtered them out. Another shot whizzed by his ear and another ibex fell. Horror-struck, Laszlo dashed to the front of the herd and cut them off. Now he would drive them *toward* the woods, to save their lives. Another shot rang out. How many did they want? Laszlo wondered. Two could feed everyone in the village for a week. Or were they after something else? A wolf, maybe?

The sound of barking grew closer. Laszlo snarled more savagely and bit harder at the ibexes' flanks. Another gunshot gave the herd the incentive they needed to reach the forest's edge. Once inside, they splintered off and, as if by magic, vanished into thin air. Laszlo then dove into the undergrowth and began weaving through it with every bit of strength and cunning he could muster. The hounds gave chase, but were no match for him. Soon Laszlo heard the voices of their masters calling them back. He didn't slow his pace, though, until he could see his flock on the flushing through the trees. Gizi was reining them in. Rita was lying on a blanket in the sun nearby, knitting.

He shot out of the forest as if it were on fire and

bounded across the field, his head up, his tongue dangling. Rita spotted him and waved an arm over her head. When Laszlo reached her, he licked at her face.

"Ibex blood," she said, when he'd calmed down. "What have you been doing?"

Laszlo wished himself a boy again and buried his head in his mother's lap.

"Tell me, my love," she said, stroking his hair. "There's nothing to fear."

He told her everything in one mad rush: about the ibex and the hunters, about the boys, the witch-burning, the whispers. He told her how Muno had seen her change. It felt good to get it all out, lying there in the ease of her lap with the sound of the grazing ewes and the feel of the cool breeze on his skin. But then afterward, when he realized what the consequences might be, his dread came surging back.

"We have to leave, don't we?" he asked.

Rita looked away at the hills, her eyes wet. "I'm afraid so," she said.

◆ ◆ ◆

To Laszlo's shock, Kalman disagreed.

"One doesn't pick up and leave in late autumn," he said. "Even if we could find a new place to live, we could never get resettled before winter sets in. We have no money and nothing much to sell, and we'd be building a sheepfold in the snow. It's been all I can do just to get the one we have in shape. We can't go. We'll have to stay and take our chances."

Even Rita was speechless. Kalman had had one foot out the door for weeks, and suddenly, with rumors in the village and an eyewitness to their shape-shifting living right under the priest's nose, he was pulling that foot back in and slamming the door.

"But just the other day were you saying —" Rita began.

"I know, I know," Kalman said. "But let's just wait awhile and see what happens. Now that Laszlo has been through the pool we can always hide in the other world, if it comes to that. The pack will shelter us until it is safe to come back for what little we own."

Laszlo thought it over and realized that his father was right. Winters were harsh in the mountains, and the last thing they would want was to roll in to a new town, homeless and penniless, and have to ask for help. Strangers were not welcome in Saint-Eustache in any season. They were always met with suspicion, especially ones who were down on their luck or spoke with an accent. There was no reason to believe any other village would be different. And finding a plot of land and building a house and fold in time for winter would be impossible. The risks of going outweighed the risks of staying, especially now that they could all slip into the "other world," as Kalman called it. Laszlo was so glad that he had been shown the door to it.

Though it seemed unlikely, Laszlo tried to believe there still was a chance no one would come for them. Maybe Muno would continue to hold her tongue. Maybe the whispers would remain just that: whispers. Maybe Laszlo hadn't changed in front of the boys. Maybe everyone would be too busy preparing for winter to bother with a family of shepherds way out in the hills. These were the only hopes Laszlo had, and he clung to them.

"I think the best thing now would be to stay out of the village," Kalman said. "That and keep our noses alert. We'll know they're coming in plenty of time to escape, provided we remain vigilant. Human beings move very slowly. They won't be hard to detect."

"No more trading?" Laszlo asked. Surely they would need bread and other things that they couldn't provide for themselves.

"Only out of desperation, and then as inconspicuously as possible. Maybe it would be better to go to Montcorbeau. It's much farther away, but safer. We can pack up and leave in the spring, once there are lambs."

Then he looked Laszlo right in the eye and said very sternly, "Don't keep things like this from us again, son.

There are no greater horrors on earth than those that go on in a church dungeon. We have kept you in the dark about much of it. But you have gone through the pool now, and it's time you knew."

He looked at Rita and she nodded her agreement.

"Your mother and I were arrested once," he went on. "It was before you were born. We were arrested merely for being strangers, because of baseless rumors. We sat in court, denied our right to speak, and listened as we were sentenced to death for crimes we never committed."

"But how —" Laszlo began.

"We escaped," Kalman said. "But we just as easily could have been caught. We've known others of our kind who could not escape. It would only have taken one error in judgment, a little bad luck, and then we would have been bound to the stake like so many have been before us. Like those poor people you saw in the village."

Laszlo shuddered. It was a horror he prayed never to see again.

"That is what we don't want to happen," Kalman went on. "We all have to do everything in our power to prevent that from ever happening. Do you understand?"

"Yes, Papa," Laszlo said, his heart aching. "I'm so sorry."

"Don't upset yourself about it, Laszlo," Rita said. "This is a confusing time for you. The change affects every part of you, not just your body. Emotions can be overwhelming. But it will get easier. You'll see." She kissed his forehead.

Laszlo nodded, letting himself take some comfort from her words, then asked, "Do you think I became a wolf in front of those boys?"

Kalman smiled. "I don't mean to scare you, son, but I doubt they would have let you live if you had. You have to be careful now. You have to remain aware of what you're thinking, what you wish for, even to yourself. Especially to yourself."

Laszlo understood. He would have to stay more alert to both the outside and the inside world.

"I will," he said. "I promise."

◆　◆　◆

No one from the village came that day, or the next. Sunday came again and went, but nothing other than icier winds visited Laszlo's fields. The time was not spent merely waiting, of course. There was much to be done. The family worked in the fields, cutting and baling hay and straw. Kalman pressed mud into the chinks in the walls of the house, the fold, and the shed, and repaired the roofs and fences. Rita mended the previous year's winter clothes, as some were badly moth-eaten. She stored the last batches of dried herbs, beans, and grains. When the sheep were in, Laszlo collected firewood, chopped it into logs, and stacked it beside the house. He also rummaged through the garden for any remaining root vegetables, planted new bulbs and seeds, and harvested wild mushrooms. These were weeks of incessant toil, but Laszlo knew that soon would come months spent indoors, so he did his best to relish those remaining days on the meadows with Gizi and the sheep. He always kept an eye, an ear, and a nostril trained for intruders. Each passing day served to ease his mind, but he did not allow his senses to ease. He maintained his vigil.

During this time, thoughts of Muno continued to haunt his mind. He couldn't bear not knowing how she was, or where. He reminded himself that he'd been instructed to forget her, and so tried to put her out of his mind. The thoughts, however, rarely obeyed.

The first frost came, then the first snowfall, and still no one had appeared. Laszlo felt a deep chill in his bones and knew that it would remain there for months. Winter meant that everything would become more difficult and everyone would have less energy, so it only seemed natural that they should spend less time working — there was less to do — and more time sitting inside by the fire. Though Laszlo preferred the freedom of the other seasons, he did enjoy curling up by the hearth with his knitting and Kalman's books.

Kalman had begun reading from the pamphlet that Laszlo had given him, the essays of Michel de Montaigne. Montaigne seemed to Laszlo like someone who had done his best throughout his life to appreciate the world around him and to respect life in all its forms.

"'We must judge with more reverence the infinite power of nature, and with more consciousness of our own ignorance and weakness,'" Kalman read one evening.

These words rang in Laszlo's head later, as he stared out at the white world. He changed to a wolf, he thought, the way the weather turns cold, then warm, the way the clouds become gray, then white, the way water becomes ice, then ice, water. To ask him to be anything else would be like asking the snow not to fall, the sun not to shine, the wolf not to howl. Nature made him what he was. Who was he, or anyone else, to judge Her work?

Père Raoul preached that werewolves were evil beings, deserving of nothing but torture and death. But Laszlo did not feel evil. He felt no diabolical forces within him, no desire to triumph over good, to rise up against God and His followers. It was true he'd felt disgust at the burning. Did that mean that he was disgusted with God? Was it God's will that people be burned at the stake? Was it possible Père Raoul was wrong about what God wanted?

And was it possible to be a werewolf and still be good?

Soon there was no longer any reason to go outside except to refill the sheep's manger and water trough, clean the fold, collect firewood, and bring in pailfuls of snow. The rest of the days and nights were spent huddled by the fire, which was perpetually lit; without it, the family would freeze. Even with it the cold was so bitter that they kept bundled up in nearly every article of clothing they owned. They slid the bed across the floor to the hearth. They nailed shut the shutters and stuffed a rug under the door to keep out drafts. Except for the fire, the clothes, and the handiwork, they were living like wolves in a den.

Then one particularly frigid January evening, Laszlo asked, "Why don't we just change?"

Rita and Kalman looked at each other, and shrugged.

"Why not indeed!" Rita said with a laugh.

"But what if someone comes by?" Kalman said.

"Oh, no one has come by in months."

"That doesn't mean someone can't knock on the door at any moment."

"Yes, but they couldn't see *in*," Rita said.

"And if we were wolves, we'd smell them," Laszlo added.

"Hm," Kalman said. "That's true enough." Then he grinned a little. "Why haven't we ever done it before?"

"Probably because it would have seemed unfair to Laszlo," Rita said. "We did it before he was born."

Kalman nodded. "That's right. I forgot. Isn't it funny how easy it is to forget things you once did every day?"

"We wolved a lot more in those days, too," Rita said, "because you worried a lot less."

"Well, the young never worry enough, do they?" Kalman said. "Young people think they're going to live forever."

"Papa," Laszlo asked, "did you want to go through the pool?" It was a question he'd long wanted to ask.

"The pool?" Kalman said.

Rita laughed. "Yes, answer him, Kalman! Tell him about when you went through. Go on. I want to relive it!"

Kalman squinted at her, and she returned the face.

"So you knew Mama before you could change?" Laszlo asked.

"I did," Kalman said wearily.

Rita snickered. "He couldn't stand the sight of me!" she said.

"That's a little strong," Kalman said. "You always exaggerate, Rita."

"Always?"

"I could stand the sight of you," he said, then smirked. "It was the *sound* of you I couldn't stand. Oh, Laszlo, she was the noisiest girl on earth."

"I wasn't noisy," Rita said somewhat crossly. "I had a lot to say. You were just the quietest boy. I couldn't get a peep out of you."

"How could you? You never stopped talking."

"You never started."

"Were you neighbors?" Laszlo interrupted.

"We grew up on the same farm in Erdély," Kalman said. "Our mothers were cousins."

"Several times removed," Rita added.

"We went through the pool at the same time, even though I'm older."

"I matured faster," Rita said.

"Did you want to go through?" Laszlo asked.

"Well, *I* did," Rita said, grinning at Kalman.

"I wasn't so sure," he said.

"Why?" Laszlo asked.

His father sighed. "There are dangers that accompany changing, son. Wolf folk are not very, well, *popular.*"

"'Popular' — ha!" Rita said. "That's putting it mildly!"

"But you said he didn't worry as much then," Laszlo said.

"He didn't, but he still worried more than most people."

"I thought I was telling this," Kalman grumbled.

"He saw me go through, and then he just dove right in," Rita said. "He didn't want me to be something he wasn't."

Kalman shrugged. "I was going to dive in. I just don't rush into things the way you do."

"Admit it, Kalman," Rita said. "You were afraid to lose me."

"I was not."

"Oh, you haven't changed a bit!"

"How did you feel afterward?" Laszlo asked. "Were you afraid?"

"I remember being afraid," Rita said with a sigh. "To be truthful, I'm still often afraid. But I don't regret it. What I've learned being a wolf has been well worth the risks."

Kalman nodded solemnly. "It has not made life easy, but it certainly has had its rewards."

Rita smiled at him, and he took her hand in his.

"So can we?" Laszlo said, trying to guide the conversation back to his original question.

"Can we what?" Kalman asked.

"Can we change?" Laszlo asked. "In the house, to stay warm?"

"I don't see why not," Rita said.

"Only in the house, of course," Kalman cautioned. "And not all the time. There is still plenty of work to do that requires hands."

"But at night?" Laszlo asked. "When we sleep?"

"Oh, it will be so much cozier!" Rita said.

"Yes, I suppose that would be all right," Kalman said uneasily.

From that night on, the family slept in their fur and let the fire go out. Rita praised Laszlo for being such a clever young man, but to Laszlo it wasn't cleverness. Trying to think of reasons to change was something he did more and more. To him, the hardest part of being cooped up had been not being allowed to become a wolf. Due to another of Kalman's bans on wolving, Laszlo hadn't changed since the day he'd herded the ibex, and he dearly longed to. He missed flying through the woods. He missed sensing all that a wolf senses. If he couldn't go out into the wild as one, at least he could go to sleep each night and awaken each morning a wolf.

CHAPTER TEN

By the end of January, the larder was empty. The family had grown as thin as the soup. Something had to be done.

"It's too dangerous to go into Saint-Eustache," Kalman said. "I'll go to Montcorbeau and try to do some trading."

"Food will be very expensive," Rita said. "It always is in the dead of winter."

"I'll bring blankets and clothing. We don't need as many now that we're changing and the demand for them will be high."

"But we'll need them, Kalman, when it gets colder. We're not wolves all day, you know."

"Maybe we'll be able to shear one of the sheep in a month or so and make more."

"It will be too late by then!"

"Well, what else can we do?"

"We could hunt," Laszlo said. "As wolves."

Rita looked at Kalman. "Well, what do you say?" she said.

Kalman had long ago set a moratorium on hunting, in either human or wolf form. Seigneur Pussort's laws of the land stated clearly that any person caught poaching in any of his forests would have their eyes put out. The several eyeless men in the village were testament to the law's enforcement. The punishment for wolves discovered hunting in the woods was, of course, even more severe.

"Absolutely not," Kalman answered.

"We could hunt at night," Rita said. "Men don't hunt after dark."

Kalman considered this, but still shook his head. "Let me go to Montcorbeau first," he said. "Maybe I can get enough food to get us through until spring without giving up too many woolens. If that doesn't work, then we'll talk about hunting."

"But what about *now?*" Rita whined.

Both Kalman and Laszlo stared at her. Rita never whined.

"What is it?" Kalman said, eyeing her carefully. "What's wrong? There's something you're not saying."

Rita scowled at him. "There's nothing wrong," she said testily. "I'm hungry."

"There are still some beans," Laszlo said.

"I don't want beans!" Rita snapped. "I want *meat!*"

Laszlo was stunned. Kalman grinned.

"So *that's* it," Kalman said.

"Just because I want meat," Rita seethed, "does not mean I'm with child!"

"When you want it that much, it does."

"Are you, Mama?" Laszlo asked.

Since Laszlo was old enough to understand what it meant, Rita had suffered two miscarriages. Before he was old enough to understand, she had given birth to two sons, neither of whom saw even a year of life, and a daughter, who was born dead. These things were never discussed by anyone. They remained hidden behind Rita's laughter.

"No," Rita answered bitterly.

"No?" Kalman said. "Honestly no?"

"I'm not pregnant," Rita said. "I ought to know by now when I am." Her brow darkened. "I'm just starving, and beans won't suffice."

Kalman held her. "Forgive my teasing," he said. "I'll get you a rabbit for your supper."

"Thank you, kind sir," Rita replied.

"Can I come?" Laszlo asked.

"Out of the question!" Kalman said.

"Let him go with you," Rita said. "He'll be fine. You worry too much."

"I have to," Kalman said. "You don't worry at all."

"Please?" Laszlo whined.

"It's like the house is full of puppies tonight!" Kalman said, throwing his hands up in the air. "All right, but listen to me, Laszlo. Even if there are no hunters, there are still traps. Stay off human trails, both the kind you see and the kind you smell, and stay close. Wolves are stronger in packs. Remember, winter is the hungry season."

"All right, Kalman," Rita said. "Enough advice and admonition. Get going, both of you."

Laszlo was a wolf before she'd finished her sentence.

♦   ♦   ♦

Half a moon hung in the indigo sky, bathing the snow-covered pastures in opalescent light. The scent of autumn had been buried in ice, replaced by the crisp, uncluttered scent of winter. Laszlo and Kalman moved in a line over the frozen snow, Laszlo's paws falling naturally into the larger prints of his father's, his toes opening up like snowshoes. Their warm breath turned to plumes of steam. A couple of times Laszlo scented small rodents under the snow, but he did as his father did: disregarded them. They needed game to feed three stomachs, perhaps several times. Mice wouldn't do.

They hunted for more than an hour without success.

Laszlo didn't mind. Had it not been for his mother's hunger, he'd have gladly stayed out all night. When finally the scent of a capercaillie found the wolves' nostrils, Kalman crouched and began creeping stealthily toward the source, Laszlo following closely in his paw prints. The bird was wandering alone along a stream, pecking at the stones on the bank. The two wolves crept stealthily to within pouncing distance, then Kalman lunged. The capercaillie let out a cackle, flapped its wings, and fluttered up off the ground just enough to elude death, at least for the moment; in the next, Laszlo sprang and caught it by the throat. It beat at his body with its wings and scratched at him with its claws. Laszlo bit down harder and tasted blood on his tongue. The bird convulsed, and Laszlo instinctively shook it from side to side, feeling its flesh tearing in his teeth. Warm blood spattered across the snow. When he stopped, the bird drooped limply in his mouth. He dropped it in a heap onto the frozen snow. Its eyes lolled. Its chest heaved. It was still alive. Laszlo scooped it up again and shook it. He could feel its small bones breaking in his teeth, hear them snapping, then once again he dropped the poor thing onto the bloodstained snow. This time it was dead. He had killed it.

The instincts of the wolf receded then, and the mind of the boy was horrified to see what he had done. He felt sickened and ashamed. He had slaughtered a live creature, and not with an ax or arrow or hook; he had broken its neck in his jaws. He worried that it was wrong to kill that way, like a beast. Were beasts and men different in the eyes of God? He hadn't killed out of anger or envy or fear. He hadn't killed the bird because it was evil. He'd killed it for his mother, because she needed food. Why did the priest burn people at the stake? Did he have some need to? Did God?

Laszlo felt a nudge on his shoulder and turned to see a large silver wolf standing beside him. How long he'd been there, Laszlo wasn't sure. Again he'd allowed his human mind to overwhelm his senses. He had forgotten his promise to remain aware of the world around him, and his father's disappointment was apparent in his eyes.

Kalman scooped up the bird in his mouth, and they set off for home. Laszlo felt a tingle of pride as he imagined how happy his mother would be to see what he had killed for her.

And his confusion started all over again.

◆　　◆　　◆

The capercaillie took the edge off Rita's hunger, at least temporarily, and since it could be frozen, it would provide enough meat for a couple of days. That gave Kalman the time he needed to go to Montcorbeau and, hopefully, do some trading. He packed up what little they had and set out the next morning. When he returned four days later, he had quite a tale to tell.

"As it turns out," he said, "Marie-France's uncle is the miller, and I don't need to tell you what that means. His house was enormous, with a kitchen and two fireplaces and stables. Yes, they had *horses!* Three of them!"

"But how did you find him?" Rita asked.

"That's a story in itself," Kalman said, clearly pleased to have been asked. "I was in the village square, practically alone there, trying to find someone interested in what I had to trade, when a fine young woman walked up to me and asked to look at a scarf. When I handed it to her, I saw she was smiling at me quite familiarly, and so naturally I smiled back. I have to admit, though, it was awkward. She was just beaming at me and wouldn't stop."

"It was Marie-France?" Laszlo asked.

"It was, though I had to pinch myself when she told me so. She had meat on her bones and a blush on her cheek. She wore jewelry and leather shoes. She looked like a new person, full of life, and so much younger! She's younger than you, Rita."

Rita and Laszlo both smiled imagining the change in Marie-France.

"Then she led me to her new home, this palace, and introduced me to her uncle, Monsieur Lamoignan, who's a widower, and just as nice as can be. Not like most millers, you know. He didn't look down his nose at me for being a shepherd. He shook my hand and offered me a seat and" — here Kalman paused for effect — "and a glass of *wine.*"

"Oh, with his money, I'm sure it was a fine one!" Rita said.

"Indeed it was. I took every exquisite sip with you in mind, my love, wishing I could be sharing it with you."

"Oh, I'm sure of it, my love," Rita teased.

"Truly, I did!" he protested, and Rita laughed at his earnestness.

"Later, the parish priest dropped in for supper. Of course, at first I was terrified, but Père Jean, who couldn't have been more than twenty, turned out to be a fine sort, cordial and educated. We talked about Virgil all through the meal. He mentioned how the bishop is displeased with his work because he hasn't executed any heretics this year. Not one burning. He won't last, of course. The church will never tolerate that."

"That's optimistic of you, husband," Rita said.

"After supper, Monsieur Lamoignan offered me lodging for the night — or for as many nights as I liked, he said — and I swear to you, I slept on a bed stuffed with *feathers.* It was so luxurious, I could barely sleep. The next day, the man bought everything I had for three times what it was worth. I argued with him over the price, and he finally agreed and gave me a smaller sum."

"Shrewd of you," Rita said.

"Then he insisted on rewarding me for bringing Marie-France back to him. I objected, saying he'd done more than enough already, but he absolutely would not take no for an answer."

At that, Kalman jumped up from the bed and rushed outside, returning a moment later with a large hemp sack. Inside it were three large loaves of bread, six game birds, two large dried salamis, several wheels of cheese, three bottles of wine, three pairs of leather slippers lined with wool, some candles, and a small wooden box sealed up with red sealing wax.

For once, Rita was speechless.

Once Laszlo had gotten over the spectacle of it, he asked, "What's in the box?"

"Ah!" Kalman said. "That's a present for you, Laszlo, from Marie-France. A special treat, she said. Open it!"

Laszlo excitedly broke the seal and pried off the lid. Inside he found an assortment of chocolate candies, each one a different shape. He closed his eyes and breathed in their sweet aroma.

"Well, don't just sniff them, wolf boy, have one!" Kalman laughed.

Laszlo smiled, plucked one out, and set it delicately on his tongue. He had never eaten chocolate before. The taste was more heavenly than its bouquet. He didn't want to chew; he wanted the candy to melt on his tongue, then ooze down his throat. He wanted the taste to last forever. His resistance melted before the chocolate did, however, and he bit down into the luscious raspberry crème inside. He insisted that Rita and Kalman share with him, but they demurred, saying the chocolates were for him.

"Small reward," Rita said, "for the great kindness you showed Marie-France. Besides, I'm keener on the wine."

Laszlo ate a second chocolate, then closed the box and hid it away.

"I want them to last," he said, and his parents understood.

Kalman then unloaded his own bag, which contained all the goods he had taken with him to Montcorbeau, the goods the miller had purchased from him.

"He said he didn't need them after all," Kalman said, "but refused to take back his money! But wait, there's more!"

"More?" Rita said. "What else could there be? You don't

happen to have another bag with one of his horses in it, do you?"

"Of course not," Kalman said seriously, and Rita laughed. "Monsieur Lamoignan told me of a property he owns on the outside of the village with a little stone cottage on it and lots of good pasture, perfect for a shepherd and his family." He paused here for effect. "He suggested we come and live there, and pay for it as we go along. What do you think of that!"

Rita's mouth fell open. "Pay for it as we go along? You mean, *own* it?"

Kalman smiled, then took her in his arms and twirled her. She pulled Laszlo into the circle and the three of them reeled round and round the room with Gizi weaving in and out of their feet, yapping and growling, until eventually they all tumbled giddily out the door and into the snow.

◆　◆　◆

Though they now had a place to go, the family held to their decision to remain until spring. The trek through the snow would be arduous, especially with pregnant ewes. In March, the ewes would be fleeced, lambed, warm, and happy, so that was when they would leave for Montcorbeau.

The snow began to melt in late February. Buds began to appear on the trees, and an occasional woodpecker could be spotted hammering tree trunks for bugs. By the middle of the month enough meadow grass was exposed to make taking the flock out worthwhile. The ewes looked enormous with their bulging fleeces and bellies — all of them, that is, except Babette. Her fleece was spotty and her womb empty. Alphonse had not settled her successfully this year, though it was possible it was not his fault. She wasn't the ewe she once was.

"Let's hope that one of the lambs this year is female," Kalman said, examining Babette's coat. "I'm afraid she's not long for this world."

Laszlo crouched down and looked into her eyes. "Maybe she'll feel better now that spring is here," he said. He gently scratched her muzzle.

Kalman sighed. "I don't think so, son. Babette has seen her share of days. Her time is coming."

Laszlo didn't want to believe it. "Hold on, girl," he whispered. "At least until we make it to Montcorbeau."

Once spring had really taken hold, Laszlo led the sheep across the fields to a small pond and dunked each of them into the water. When they returned to the farm, their fleeces washed, Laszlo and his parents got out their shearing blades and sharpened them on flat stones to a razor's keenness. They then stepped into Alphonse's pen and, after a rather comical chase, cornered and caught him. Kalman flipped him over onto his back on a heavy cloth and yanked him up into a sitting position. Alphonse protested, bleating noisily and flailing his legs about. He had never become accustomed to the blades. Kalman clipped his hooves first, then started snipping carefully around the brisket. Once it was shorn, he moved more quickly over the belly wool, his blades making a quick *zeecha-zeecha* sound. After the belly, he went around the dock, down the legs, up over the other shoulder, then, moving swiftly again, he sheared Alphonse's other side. The fleece came off in one piece. Kalman tossed it aside, calling, "Wool away!"

Henriette, who was far more compliant, was next. While Rita sheared her, Laszlo and Kalman picked clumps of dirt and debris — twigs, hay, dried manure — out of Alphonse's fleece. The wool was still warm to the touch. The lanolin made Laszlo's fingertips smooth and shiny, as if he'd had his hands in fresh butter.

"Wool away!" Rita yelled, and tossed Henriette's fleece aside.

Laszlo sheared Babette while Rita and Kalman picked through Henriette's wool. Babette's fleece was thin and marred by holes. Its crimp was loose, its fibers coarser than previous years. It did not come off in one piece.

"Wool away!" Laszlo called.

Rita sheared Pernette while Laszlo and Kalman cleaned Babette's fleece. They broke for lunch before making a go at Claudette, who was the jumpiest of the bunch, worse even than Alphonse. It took all three of them to keep her still.

"Wool away!" Kalman grunted when finally she was shorn.

"Thank heaven," Rita groaned.

When they finished carding the wool late that afternoon, they had a bundle of five fleeces ready for spinning, a job Rita and Laszlo would share over the following weeks. Then, since the sheep had not been fed that day, Laszlo took them out to pasture. As they went along he noticed that both Henriette and Pernette kept pawing at the ground and bleating in anxious voices. Once out on the meadow, they barely ate at all. Their udders were red and swollen. It wouldn't be long before there would be lambs in the fold.

The day was glorious, so bright and warm that Laszlo felt compelled to run in circles around the flock, his arms outstretched like wings, his head flung back, howling at the sun. When his pent-up energy was spent, he lay back on the grass, listening to his happy sheep munching, thinking of his rosy new future. The family had survived the winter. No one had come for them. They had fleeces and food and a new home to go to. There they'd have friends. True, they'd be leaving home, a prospect that, before, had kept Laszlo from revealing a dreadful secret, but they'd also be leaving Père Raoul, the dungeon, the stake, and the whispers. They'd be going to a village with a kindly priest and friendly faces. To Laszlo, the benefits outweighed the losses.

When the light grew soft and pink, Laszlo led the flock back to the farm, his hand on Babette's neck the whole way. When he spied the mound of granite boulders behind which he'd first spied Muno, his thoughts mired in memories of her. Over the long winter months he'd become more proficient at dismissing thoughts of her, but this day, due perhaps to his more hopeful, confident mood, he allowed himself to linger over them. His mind ran backward over his few encounters with her, nearly all of which had been fraught with distress and conflict. Even so, he missed her terribly, and would have done anything — short of imperiling his family — to be reassured that she was well and free. He had respected Muno's, and his father's, wishes, and stayed away, but his concern for her was not as easily banished. She was out of his life, but not out of his mind.

Neither Kalman nor Rita were outside when Laszlo

reached the farm. He assumed Rita was in the house, making supper. Kalman was probably drawing water from the stream, or collecting firewood. Or maybe they were together in the house. Sometimes they took short naps while Laszlo was out with the sheep. They would hang a clog on the door in case he returned while they were resting. The clog meant they did not want to be disturbed. There was no clog.

Gizi started to growl.

"What is it?" Laszlo said, sniffing the air.

He had been so deep in his thoughts of Muno that he had let his guard drop. He inhaled deeply . . . and smelled men! They were nearby, and Kalman was out alone!

"Mama!" he yelled, running for the house, Gizi at his side barking furiously. He pushed the door open, then froze at the sight of Père Raoul, standing by the hearth, wearing his biretta and long black coat. Two men, both gendarmes from the village, had Kalman's arms pinned behind him. A skein of yarn was stuffed into his mouth. Gendarmes also held Rita. She, too, was gagged. Two more men whom Laszlo recognized as gravediggers stepped forward and grabbed his arms. Gizi snapped at one of them, catching the cloth of his trousers, and the man swiftly withdrew a cudgel from his waistband and brought it down on the dog's head. She fell to the floor without a whimper. A stream of blood oozed from her ear.

147

CHAPTER ELEVEN

Before they were ushered out of the house, Laszlo and his parents were ordered to disrobe and given tunics bearing yellow crosses. The tunics were made of wool far too coarse for garments, the sort generally used for rugs or sacks, and smelled as if they had never been washed. Still, neither the discomfort of wearing one nor of having a ball of yarn stuffed into his mouth registered with Laszlo. His body was too numbed by panic, his mind too swamped with fear and regret. The knowledge that what was happening was his fault was accompanied by images of his mother and father, hooded, emaciated, bruised, and shivering in terror as they awaited the meting out of Père Raoul's cruel penance. Laszlo would stand behind the priest as well, facing the cheering, bloodthirsty crowd, watching as they gathered wood and raised a stake.

If only he had told his parents before winter had set in, he told himself, they could have fled. It would have been difficult, but not impossible. Why had he waited? Because of all that he had stood to lose? But what did he stand to lose now? He should have told his parents immediately that Muno had seen Rita change. Why hadn't he?

For a moment he blamed Muno. It was her fault for running away that day, for being there to see what she'd seen, and for telling what she'd seen. Laszlo felt certain that she had told, though undoubtedly under the strain of torture. Had there been no Muno there would have been no suspicion, no arrest. His family would not be suffering. It was all because of her.

But he knew in his heart this was not true. She surely did not intend to see what she saw that day on the flushing, and it had not been her responsibility to tell Laszlo's parents what she'd seen. It had been his. He knew that if there was anyone to blame, it was himself.

As Père Raoul's men led them, bound and gagged, down the path toward the village, the terror roiling in Laszlo's mind poured out into his body, into his belly, into his limbs. His knees buckled several times before finally folding up under him. He fell forward onto the ground on his hands and vomited. The gravediggers yanked him back up and pulled him onward. His clogs slipped off, leaving his bare feet to drag in the dirt.

When they passed the swineherd's farm, the pigs began squealing and the swineherd hollered, "A good day's work, Father! I always knew one day I'd see that lot in chains!"

Père Raoul raised his hand and said solemnly, "'And the shepherds shall have no way to flee, nor the principal of the flock to escape.' The Lord looks after his children, my son."

"Amen, Father," the swineherd said, and bowed his head.

◆　　◆　　◆

When they reached the village, one of the gendarmes knocked at the gate. "Open up!" he demanded.

Egmont peered through his little window. "Oh, yes, Father!" he said. "Right away, Father!" He pulled the door open. "Why, you've got the Embereks, Father. There must be some mistake."

"These shepherds are friends of yours, gatekeeper?" Père Raoul said.

"Well, yes, Father," Egmont said. "Acquaintances, that is. I let them in and out, like I let all friends in and out."

"Well, in the future I advise you to choose your friends more judiciously," the priest said. "And keep to your duties.

It is not your place to question the judgment of the seigneur's court."

"No, Father," Egmont said, looking down. "I apologize, Father."

As Laszlo was dragged away, he peered back over his shoulder, praying that Egmont would never see consequences from that small act of loyalty.

The trial took place in the tavern. The petty judge sat at a heavy wooden table — the sort difficult to overturn during drunken brawls — and was flanked by Père Raoul and a curate. Laszlo and his parents stood facing the three of them, their hands locked in shackles. Other than the gendarmes and the gravediggers, no one else was present in the room. The judge cleared his throat and adjusted his bone-framed spectacles. He was a very old man, one of more than fifty years, and wore a black cloak not unlike Père Raoul's. His hair was almost gone, his face plump and ruddy, with drooping bags under his eyes and loose, flapping jowls. His lips were tightly drawn, as if he held something bitter in his mouth. Laszlo had often seen the man with members of the Fabric but was uncertain whether he was a member himself. He had also seen him at the patronal festival, laughing and cavorting with Père Raoul and Seigneur Pussort. He was not laughing now.

"Kalman Emberek, Rita Emberek, Laszlo Emberek," he said, "you have been accused by several citizens of fine standing in this community of practicing black magic. One gentlewoman has claimed that she had borne two healthy sons before first buying milk and cheese from you, but that since that time her womb has been barren. A friend of hers, also of honorable standing, has testified that she, too, has been unable to conceive since purchasing milk from you four years ago."

"I beg your pardon, your honor, but these honorable women have sought the participation of their good husbands, I presume," Rita said. "Surely the good women have not been trying to conceive in the manner of the Blessed Virgin."

The judge gave her a stern look. "I'll have no impertinence in my court, madame, especially from a witch. It would be in your best interest to take this matter very seriously."

Laszlo sighed. That would not be easy for Rita.

"I beg your pardon, sir," she said with a false note of contrition in her voice. "And it has not been proven that I am a witch, sir."

"You will hold your tongue, madame!" the judge said. "If you persist in speaking out of turn I shall have no alternative but to condemn you on the spot!"

Kalman elbowed Rita in the ribs and she returned the jab.

Laszlo's heart pounded in his throat. He wished for once his mother could silence her irreverence. With all that was at stake, how could she be so reckless?

"Yes, your honor," she said.

"Furthermore," the judge went on, "a gentleman who last autumn purchased a cloak made from your wool suffered from terrible boils all winter long. The man's son also claims that, during a recent altercation with your son, he broke a toe."

"Excuse me, your honor," Rita said, "but I'm confused. *Who* broke a toe?"

"The gentleman's son," the judge said.

"And whose did he break?"

"Why, his own, of course," snapped the curate. "It was plainly put in the man's deposition."

Rita looked down at the dirt floor. "Forgive me, but I am only an ignorant shepherd's wife, sir. Which is not to imply that my husband is an ignorant shepherd." She gave Kalman another jab.

"Guard!" the judge said. "Take this woman away at once and lock her in a cell where she can no longer profane this holy place!"

"I was not aware, your honor," Rita said as one of the gendarmes grasped her arm, "that the Lord consecrated taverns."

"The Lord," Père Raoul interjected, "consecrates right-eousness wherever it resides."

As he watched Rita being led away, a terror gripped Laszlo. Would he never see her again? He grew dizzy and began to totter, but Kalman caught him by the arm.

"With your permission, your honor —" Kalman began.

"You may not speak!" the judge said, his palm upraised. "This court is not in the practice of hearing the pleas of witches. A witch's tongue is moved by the Devil, and I will not waste this court's time indulging Satan's lies and deceit."

This logic confounded Laszlo's already addled mind. His father was not a witch, yet he could not say that he was not, because, since witches were liars, any word in his own defense would be considered further proof of his guilt. The only admissible thing Kalman — or Rita or Laszlo himself — could do was to agree with the court that they were witches, which they weren't. In other words, the truth was judged false, and falsehood, true. No wonder Rita had resorted to mockery. The situation was absurd.

"Furthermore," the judge went on, "the parish priest, Père Raoul, reports that a person — a young girl who by her own admission has practiced black arts against this community — has named you, sir, and your family as members of her very own coven, and that you, sir, are in fact the lord of that coven." He glared at Kalman scornfully.

Kalman did not speak. He only straightened up and returned the glare. But Laszlo could keep silent no longer.

"It isn't true!" he shouted. "We *aren't* witches! We don't practice black magic — *you* do! In your dungeons, in the square, *you* make people suffer. You burn people at the stake. You tortured Muno into confessing. *You* are the devils!"

The judge rose immediately from his chair without even a glance in Laszlo's direction. He addressed Kalman.

"Once we have the names of your consorts, sir, you and your family will be properly punished before this community and before our Lord, whom your wife and son have so blasphemed." Then he turned to Père Raoul and said in a lower tone, "I want their confessions."

"You will have them, your honor," Père Raoul said.

◆   ◆   ◆

The dungeon guard unlocked the door, then, with his help, the gendarmes clamped Laszlo's wrists and ankles into iron shackles that hung from the walls of the cell. The wrist cuffs were situated so that Laszlo's arms hung diagonally upward from his shoulders, his hands flopping lamely forward. The wall at his back was made of cold, damp stone. The gendarmes chained his parents to the opposite wall, then left the cell. The guard shut it and locked the door behind them, plunging the room into darkness.

"What gets into you?" Kalman hissed.

"The man was an imbecile," Rita said. "What chance did we have with him? We were convicted before we were arrested. That wasn't a trial. It was a formality. You heard him. He called me a witch. I had no interest in sitting there and listening to his sanctimonious playacting. You know as well as I do what those courts are. No witnesses. No jury."

"Well, there's no point in arguing," Kalman said. "They'll be coming for us soon."

"Will they t-torture us?" Laszlo said.

"No," Rita said firmly, "for the simple fact that we won't be here. We're leaving."

Of course! Laszlo thought. In his fear, he'd forgotten that his parents had been arrested, and had escaped, before.

"Honestly, I've never understood the logic of locking up witches," Rita went on. "How do you keep a sorceress in chains? Wouldn't she merely transform herself into a bee or something? No dungeon in the world could hold a bee!"

And she changed. Being vertical made freeing herself cumbersome, but after a moment or two of writhing she slipped her paws through the shackles and fell forward onto the floor, her tunic still draped over her torso.

"We'll growl until the guard gets suspicious and opens the door," Kalman whispered to Laszlo, "then we'll jump him. He'll be so taken aback, it won't be hard to get past him. But that's just the beginning. The hard part will be getting out of town. Your mother seems to think that there's nothing to it, but she tends to forget how ruthless men like Père Raoul can be. I would have preferred to try to talk our way out of this, but your mother had different ideas."

Rita growled at him.

"But if we are careful and use our advantage — our senses, our speed, the element of surprise — we will escape. Do you understand, son?"

"Y-Yes, Papa," Laszlo said.

Kalman changed, shook free of his shackles, then landed beside Rita. They tore at each other's tunics with their teeth and claws until they were rid of them.

Laszlo worried for a moment that he wouldn't be able to change, that under the circumstances he'd never be able to concentrate hard enough. But he wanted nothing less right then than to be a human being, to be related to the judge and the priest and the villagers who had stepped up to condemn them, to be one of a species that treated its own so cruelly. He wanted to be as his parents were — and he became a wolf. He wriggled free of his chains and fell to the floor between them. They ripped his tunic to pieces, then began to growl. In no time the smell of the guard grew stronger, the sound of his footsteps down the corridor louder. Laszlo was pleased to detect alcohol on the man's breath and an irregularity in his step. His drunkenness meant he would be easier to overcome.

The key rattled in the lock, then a silhouette of the guard's hunched figure appeared in the doorway. Kalman was upon him in an instant. The man uttered a startled grunt, then stumbled backward under the enormous wolf's force. Rita sprang at him as well and the extra push drove him back out into the corridor, where his head knocked against the stone wall. His body went slack and slumped to the floor. Kalman changed, removed the ring of keys from the man's hand, then leaned in close to his face.

"He's breathing," he whispered, then picked up the guard's torch.

And that was when a familiar scent reached Laszlo's nostrils. He knew what it was instantly and quickly returned to human form.

"It's Muno!" he whispered. "I smell her! She's nearby. She knows the way out. She helped Marie-France escape, remember?"

Kalman nodded. "Lead the way," he said.

Laszlo became a wolf again and tracked the scent down the corridor. Rita, still a wolf, padded after him, with

Kalman bringing up the rear. Laszlo stopped at a door and sniffed under it. Muno was behind it. Laszlo whined and scratched at the floor. Kalman tried a key, then another, until he struck on the right one. He pushed the door open, and Laszlo, already human again, rushed inside.

"*Muno!*" he whispered. "It's me, Laszlo!"

There was no reply.

Kalman stepped inside and the torch filled the tiny cell with light. Muno was shackled to the wall, just as Laszlo and his parents had been, her body hanging limp as a scarecrow, her head drooping lifelessly. Her scalp was covered with patchy black stubble, her arms and legs etched with thin, black scabs. Impossibly, she was thinner than before.

"Muno," Laszlo said more gently. He touched her arm. Her skin was ice cold. Fear seized him, and he shook her. "*Muno!*"

Her head lifted on its own ever so slightly, then dropped again.

Laszlo sighed. "Come with us," he said. "We need your help."

Kalman unlocked her shackles, then hoisted her over his shoulder like a sack of grain.

"Which way, Muno?" he asked.

"Left," she said in a thin rasp.

They followed her directions through the maze of tunnels, turning left or right as she instructed. Every word she spoke seemed to revive her more.

"There's a tunnel that runs under the village," she said when they reached a dead end. "To reach the entrance we must pass through the church."

"Through the *church?*" Kalman gasped.

"It's the only way," Muno said.

"How do we get into the church?" Laszlo asked.

"Through there," she said, and pointed at a trapdoor over their heads. A wooden ladder leaned against the wall below it.

"There's someone up there," Laszlo said, sniffing the air.

Rita regained her human form. "I smell it, too," she said.

Kalman inhaled deeply. "It's not the priest. I smell soap."

"The door opens behind the confessional," Muno said. "It's locked, but you have the key. Open it a crack. If it's safe, go straight to the seigneur's door."

"The seigneur's door!" Kalman said.

Rita took the keys from him and climbed the ladder. She tried several of them before finding the right one, then pushed the door up just enough to peek through.

"There's a woman scrubbing the floor," she whispered. "She's between us and the seigneur's door."

"That's Ghislaine," Muno said. "She won't bother us. She's simple. Does she have a lantern?"

"Yes," Rita said.

"Take it as you go by. It will be dark in the tunnel."

"Won't she tell someone she saw us?" Kalman asked.

"The poor thing doesn't even know her own name," Muno said. "The key to the seigneur's door is bronze and has his coat of arms engraved into it. Find it and have it ready."

"Here it is," Rita said.

She pushed the door open wider and they all climbed out into the church. Being last, Laszlo closed the door behind him. Since Kalman still held Muno, and Rita had the torch, Laszlo scooped up Ghislaine's lantern. She was on her hands and knees and looked up at him as he took it, her face round and flat with a large jaw and small, wide-set eyes. She appeared unable to make any sense of him, as if she had never seen a person before. There was something so innocent about her that Laszlo paused.

"We need the lantern, madame," he whispered politely to her. "I'm sorry."

A broad, open, toothless smile spread across her face, transforming it from befuddlement to elation.

"*Laszlo!*" Kalman hissed.

Laszlo turned and saw that Rita had already opened the seigneur's door. He hurried away, leaving Ghislaine behind in the darkness.

"Lock it," Muno said when they had all passed through. "Then hurry. This is no place to be caught."

Rita relocked the door and they scurried away down a corridor. Its floor was laid with flat, shiny stones; a long, crimson carpet stretched over them. Sconces with unlit candles hung along the walls between paintings in heavy, ornate frames. Most of the paintings depicted gentlemen in fine clothes on horseback cradling or firing their rifles, their wolfhounds leading the way.

"There," Muno whispered. She pointed at a large wooden armoire against the wall. "Slide it away."

Laszlo and Rita set down their lights. The torch was nearly out. They pushed the armoire away, the scraping sound it made against the stones making them wince, and discovered a hole in the wall behind it. Muno didn't have to say what to do. Laszlo grabbed the lantern and led the way into the tunnel. It wasn't tall enough for him to stand in, but he found he could walk if hunched over. The tunnel first sloped downward, then leveled off, then sloped upward.

"Père Raoul will see the trapdoor unlocked," Muno whispered as they walked, "and assume we entered the church and fled into the town. So first they'll search the village. That will give us some time. If nobody comes down the seigneur's corridor, that is, and sees the armoire moved. What day is it today?"

"Thursday, thank heaven," Rita said.

"But if they discover that we've freed you," Laszlo said,

"they'll assume you have led us out of town. Père Raoul must be aware that you know where the tunnels are."

Muno nodded. "He knows."

"We're wasting time," Kalman said.

When they reached another door, Rita unlocked it, and they stepped out into the world again. Laszlo breathed in deeply, then exhaled a cloud of mist. He had thought he would never breathe fresh air again. The moon and stars glimmered overhead. They never looked more beautiful.

Kalman leaned over Laszlo's shoulder and blew out the lantern.

"We're not free yet," he whispered. "Keep moving."

CHAPTER TWELVE

Gizi was lying on her side under the bed beside the cold hearth when they arrived home. The only part of her that moved when they stepped inside were her eyes. The fur on her head and ears was caked with dark, dried blood. Laszlo ran toward her.

"Don't touch her!" Kalman said. "Injured dogs can snap, even at their masters. Wait for her to come to you."

Laszlo sat on the ground a few feet away and waited, his heart in his throat.

Kalman laid Muno on the bed, while Rita brought her some food and water.

"Eat slowly, dear," she said softly. "Little bites, little sips."

Muno took two small bites of cheese, then fell fast asleep.

"I'll get the sheep and the cart ready," Kalman said as he pulled on a tunic. "Pack up only what we absolutely need, and quickly. There's no telling how long it will take for them to discover we're gone."

Rita began stuffing their belongings into grain sacks — food mostly, but also yarn, needles, the shearing blades, their few garden tools, and their books. She left the heavy soup pot on its hook.

"Laszlo," Kalman said, running back into the house, "Alphonse won't budge. See what you can do."

Laszlo looked up and tears streamed down his cheeks.

"Don't worry," Rita said. "I'll tend to Gizi."

While Laszlo pleaded with Alphonse, Kalman carried out first Muno, then Gizi, then the sacks. When finally Alphonse relented, Laszlo tethered him and the ewes to the back of the cart. Kalman got in front to pull, Laszlo and Rita behind to push, and they were off.

They stopped on the flushing so that the flock could fill their bellies before the long trip ahead, and Laszlo looked out over the fields glowing in the moonlight, realizing that it would very likely be the last time he ever would. They had fled the house in such a hurry that he had not even peeked back over his shoulder for one last look. The little thatched-roof house had been like a second skin that had always kept him safe and warm. He knew every inch of it, every stone, every crack, and yet he had not even bid it adieu. Nor had he to the fold, to the garden, to the oak tree his family had planted in honor of his stillborn sister. Without a parting glance, he had sped away from the farm where he'd learned to shepherd and shear and spin, perhaps because he couldn't bear to admit to himself that he would never see it again.

He walked over to his lone beech tree, and when he touched its cool bark, tears again flooded his eyes.

"We're together," Rita said, stepping up beside him. "We're alive. That's what matters most."

"It isn't right!" he cried out, his fists clenched. "None of this is right! Why is this happening?"

When his anger had ebbed, Rita wrapped her arm around him and rocked him back and forth.

"It isn't right," she said in a soft voice. "What goes on in that village in the name of God goes against everything natural in the world, and it is certainly not the only village that abides such injustice. Your father and I, our parents, and theirs, and countless generations before them have lived in many such villages in many different lands all over the world, and each time we hope for fairness and respect for life, but each time we find just the opposite. There have been terrible plagues that have extinguished countless lives all over Europe, but perhaps the worst has been the one people have brought upon themselves: the plague of human cruelty.

"You must remember that the men who pursue us,

Laszlo, no longer rely on their senses. They have lost them. They don't know what is all around them. They've lost touch with their nature. They believe they are superior to it, that God has made them so, but I see God more in the leaves of a tree, or in the eyes of a wolf, than I do in such murderous men. I do not believe it is God that motivates their actions. It is fear."

Rita paused to breathe in the fragrant night air of the meadow.

"All we can do, my love, is live by our wits and our senses, avoid danger when possible, and fight off predators, just as every creature of the world must. No place is truly safe for any living thing. Life is fragile and fraught with risks, but it is worth struggling to protect. It is the most precious thing we will ever know." She kissed his brow. "No one knows that more than a parent."

As so many times before, the warmth of his mother's embrace and the wisdom of her words soothed him. Through her he felt anchored to the world, like a tree by its roots, for through her he had entered the world, had thrived in it, had grown to adulthood. She had given him life and shown him how to live it, and she was right — it was worth protecting.

"We need to get going," Kalman said. "Laszlo, see if you can get Alphonse moving again."

Laszlo reluctantly left his mother's arms and gave Alphonse a pat on the rump. "Come on, sheep," he said.

Alphonse reluctantly took a step.

◆　◆　◆

Laszlo was much relieved when they reached the forest's edge. They knew the forest far better than anyone in the village did, including its owner, Seigneur Pussort. They also had friends there.

"I'll go and find Fridrik," Kalman said once they were well inside. "We'll need the pack's help."

As soon as he dropped to his paws he let out a long, soulful howl. A moment later there came a reply and he sprinted away.

Laszlo was sure the wolves would come to their aid once again, and wondered whether it would be the last time they'd ever be asked. In Montcorbeau, they would no longer be neighbors. The thought saddened him deeply, until it occurred to him that, considering how much ground wolves cover, it was possible that the pack's territory actually reached Montcorbeau. For human beings, it was a two-day walk; for a wolf, an afternoon jaunt. Laszlo hoped the wolf pack considered the woods around Montcorbeau home.

Laszlo assumed his father's place in front of the cart and, with Rita pushing, kept it moving along the path. Nothing — not the howling or the bumps and lurches of the cart — disturbed Muno and Gizi sleeping inside it.

When Kalman returned, he became a man again. A nervous one.

"There are men coming," he said. "They're armed and they have dogs. They're still far behind us, about midway between the village and the farm, but they can move much faster than we can with this cart. Fridrik will do what he can to slow them down, but he has his own interests to protect." He looked at Rita. "Agnes has been digging her nesting den. She'll be delivering soon."

"So will Henriette and Pernette," Laszlo said.

"Well, thank heaven you were wrong about *my* condition," Rita said to Kalman. "There are more than enough mothers-to-be in these woods tonight."

Kalman returned to the helm and they pressed on. Alphonse continued his stubbornness and in time had to be loaded into the cart with the others. This had the effect of rendering progress nearly imperceptible.

"It's still better than stopping every few minutes to plead with him," Kalman said with disgust.

Babette was next to falter. She had difficulty finding her

footing, stumbled often, bleated pitiably, then at last just sat down on the ground.

"We can't haul another one," Kalman said. "Aside from everything else, there isn't any more room in the cart."

"We have to stop, Kalman," Rita said. "It'll do us no good to inch along like this, and if we're found, there will be no escaping. Let's find a hiding place until morning. You and I can stand watch, lead the men away if they come close. Fridrik will help us."

"Yes," Kalman said. "Why don't you seek him out. There's a cave beyond this hill. I'll start us toward it."

"I know the one," Rita said. She changed and ran away into the dark.

With some kind words of encouragement, Laszlo got Babette back up on her feet and they set off for the cave. Getting over the hill proved to be a larger task than Laszlo had expected, however. His whole existence boiled down to his next step and another quarter crank of the cartwheels. The day had been exhausting and what he wanted more than anything was to climb into the cart with the dog, the ram, and the girl and escape into sleep. But he didn't. He couldn't. He kept pushing. Rita soon returned and got back behind the cart with him, but it was a long, slow slog.

When at long last they came to the top of the hill, Laszlo

and Rita moved around to the front with Kalman and the three of them guided the cart down into the valley below. The cave was well-concealed by a sprawling bracken of ferns.

"If the cart fits, it's perfect," Kalman said.

Getting the cart through the bracken wasn't easy, but once it was through, it slid neatly into the cave. Everyone let out a deep sigh.

"I'll go out on watch," Kalman said. "Rita, stay here and guard the cave. Laszlo, keep inside and tend to Muno and the animals."

"Yes, Papa," Laszlo said.

"Wait!" Rita said. *"Listen!"*

The pack had been howling ever since Kalman had first consulted with Fridrik — it was how the wolves kept track of one another — but the tone of the howls had suddenly changed. It was mournful now, grieving.

"Even Fridrik is crying," Kalman said.

"You don't think . . ." Rita began, her hand over her heart.

"No," Kalman said. "Finding a wolf den is no simple thing, and Fridrik would surely have protected it with his life."

"One of the others, then," Laszlo said. "One of the pups." He shuddered at the thought.

"We'd better go see what's happening," Rita said.

"We?" Kalman said. "One of us should stay close to the cave."

"The pack will need all the help they can get," Rita said. "Laszlo can take care of things here." And before her husband could protest, she dropped her tunic and changed.

"Stay in the cave, son," Kalman said, pulling off his clothes. "And be alert. We'll be back as soon as we can." He changed, too, then he and Rita disappeared into the woods.

"Where are we?" Muno asked in a groggy voice.

"In a cave, in the woods," Laszlo whispered. "Two of the sheep couldn't go any farther, so we decided to stop for the night. One of them is sleeping beside you. Gizi is on your other side. She's injured. There are men in the woods. I imagine Père Raoul is leading them. We heard the crying of the wolves, so my parents went out to see what was wrong."

He waited for her to ask questions — surely she would have a hundred of them — but she said nothing. He asked her if she'd like something to eat and she nodded, so he dug into one of the sacks and found a wheel of cheese.

"Thank you," she said as he gave her a piece.

"Eat slowly," Laszlo said, remembering his mother's instructions.

Her chewing slowed. When her mouth was empty, she spoke.

173

"Père Raoul threw me back into the dungeon that day in the village," she said in a low voice. "That day I saw you. He said he had finished trying to save my soul. He asked me to confess that I was a witch, like my mother and father, and he asked me to denounce you. I refused, so I was tortured."

"You don't have to tell me this," Laszlo interrupted. In truth, it was more than he could bear hearing.

"I want to," she said firmly. "I want you to know why I did what I did." She paused a second, took a breath, then went on.

"I was given nothing to eat or drink for two days. I wasn't allowed to sleep. They forced me to stand. When I'd begin to droop, they'd whip me. Then they hoisted me up into the air, facedown, a rope attached to each of my hands and feet."

Laszlo closed his eyes, but it didn't stop him from seeing what she described. He wanted her to stop, but he knew he couldn't ask again. He knew he had to listen.

"When I wouldn't confess, they shook the ropes. I thought for sure my arms would rip off at the shoulders, or my bones would shatter. But they didn't. They just felt like they would, for a very long time. When finally they let me down, they asked me again to confess. I refused. They told me they would have to hoist me again."

She looked away and said nothing for quite a while. Her

breathing was quick and raspy. Then she said, "I couldn't let them. So I lied. I said I was a witch. They asked me about your father. They wanted me to say he was a witch. I said what they wanted me to say. Then they gave me a crust of bread and a sip of water and locked me away in the dungeon."

An anger arose in Laszlo then, the strength of which he had never known, even in court. He saw himself smashing in Père Raoul's skull with a stone, ripping his throat out with his fangs, tearing him limb from limb. Laszlo had never felt anything close to this before, had never fantasized about harming anyone or anything, and it frightened him. He felt as if there were places hidden within him that he did not know existed — dark, violent places.

"I'd kill Père Raoul if I could," Muno said through her teeth.

Instead of fueling Laszlo's ire, Muno's words somehow softened it. Perhaps seeing the hatred in her eyes reminded Laszlo of the hatred he had seen in the eyes of the villagers, of the judge, and of Père Raoul, and remembering how that hatred had terrified him, his own melted away.

"'Do good to them that hate you,'" Laszlo said.

Muno closed her eyes tightly, as if trying to wipe them clean of memories. "'And pray for them which despitefully use you, and persecute you,'" she said.

"Muno," Laszlo said. He was not sure whether this was

175

the time for this question, but he had to ask. "Over and over you escaped, and yet every time, Père Raoul spared you. Why?"

To Laszlo's surprise, a wry grin flashed across her face.

"The man is utterly alone," she said. "He has no wife, of course, no children, but he also has no friends, not real ones. The seigneur uses him to maintain order. The others — the merchants, the Fabric — curry his favor, but they envy him, distrust him, fear him. They're cordial to him because their money and influence wouldn't save them if he saw fit to condemn them. The wealthy seldom burn, but it is not unheard of. I've seen rich people tied to the stake, their money and property seized by the church. They scream when the fire catches them, same as anyone."

Laszlo winced at the coldness of her remark. There was a hardness to Muno that could be chilling.

"So they show the priest respect, pay their tithes, donate their pigs, but the truth is they hate him. Everyone in the village does. They hate him because they fear his judgment. I hate him, too. But I don't fear him."

"You don't?"

"No. He destroyed my family. He took my freedom, my dignity. There is nothing left for him to take, therefore I have nothing left to fear."

Laszlo nodded to himself. Surely, losing all of one's loved

176

ones would be worse than losing one's own life. What would his life be without his parents, Gizi, the flock? If one man was responsible for such devastating losses, it made sense that one's grief, and anger, would overcome one's fear.

"Maybe the reason he's kept me around is because I've never begged him for mercy. I've never begged him for anything. He's held me prisoner, and tortured me, but he has never had me under his control. He knows that more than anything I have wanted to escape him. Death would be better than living beside him. So he controls me by keeping me alive, and at his heel — the worst punishment of all."

"You're away from him now," Laszlo said. "You'll never have to go back."

Again, Muno grinned. "You don't know him the way I do. He'll find me. He always does."

This sank the two of them into dark, dreadful thoughts, and while they brooded, Pernette began to bleat, loud and throaty. Henriette soon chimed in, then Alphonse stood up beside Muno and outdid them all. Laszlo tried shushing them, but it had no effect.

"What's wrong?" Muno said over the din. "Is someone coming?"

"No, its Pernette," Laszlo said. "She's going to give birth."

He stroked Pernette's head and cooed to her, but she was too agitated to calm down. Laszlo loosened the lead from around her neck and she quickly retreated to the inner recesses of the cave. Before long she had stopped her protesting and, as before, the others followed her cue. The cave was quiet again.

"This will be her first," Laszlo said. "She's only a year old herself. She'll be fine, though, you'll see."

Suddenly he sniffed at the air. "I smell one of the wolves. It's Agnes and Fridrik's daughter, Klotild. She is very close. That may mean the men are, too. I want to find out."

He started to undress, then stopped. "Could you please look the other way?" he asked, red-faced.

"You didn't look away that night at your house," Muno replied.

"No, I didn't," he said. He turned his back to her and dropped his cloak. "I won't be gone long. Talk softly to Pernette sometimes. Tell her everything will be fine. She likes that. Say 'Sheep, sheep, sheep.'"

"I will," Muno said.

Laszlo fell forward and changed. Muno watched, astonished, but not afraid. Laszlo the wolf pierced the bracken and bounded away.

Pernette continued to fuss.

"Everything will be fine," Muno whispered to her. "Sheep, sheep, sheep."

Laszlo quickly picked up Klotild's scent, then that of her brother, Daniel, but he could not locate the third pup, Zoltan, the brash one. Moving deeper into the woods he scented Rita, Kalman, and Fridrik, who were together and moving rapidly. He couldn't scent Agnes or her sister, Rozsa. He smelled the men and their hounds. They were scattered, running in different directions, as if panicked. Laszlo could actually hear the bated breathing of some of them. He also heard screams and gunshots. Arrows were stuck into tree trunks and into the ground. He soon picked up the scent of wolf blood, then of human blood, and then he heard the low moaning of a man. The man was moving slowly, he was bleeding, and he was not far away. As Laszlo drew closer to him, the unmistakable perfume of incense joined the strong mixture of smells.

Père Raoul.

The rage in Laszlo's breast flamed anew as he shot through the trees in the direction of the priest. He topped a hill and heard the rushing of a mountain stream. The scent of the incense, and the blood, became very strong. He could scent no other men, wolves, or dogs nearby. He sprinted down the slope and came upon the stream, which had been swollen from snowmelt. There, lying on his side on the near shore, writhing in pain, was Père Raoul. The smell of blood trailed away from him into the woods, and Laszlo spied a long, freshly carved rut in the dirt. The priest's coat was muddy and littered with debris. Clearly he had dragged himself to the stream with his hands. And then Laszlo saw why: dug into Père Raoul's bloody ankle were the jaws of a wolf trap.

Laszlo padded in closer but remained out of the priest's sight. He marveled at how easy it was to sneak up on him. This was how far removed men had become from their senses: a wolf pouncing distance away and Père Raoul was completely oblivious to it. Laszlo wondered if, in the past, he himself had ever been in a similar situation.

Père Raoul reached the surging stream and frenziedly splashed water onto his face. Without his noticing, his biretta dropped off and floated away downstream. Laszlo moved in closer, brazenly out in the open now, wondering whether he'd be able to go up and touch the man with his snout without being detected. But then all at once the priest whirled around, his face dripping, his eyes wide with terror, his breath short and sharp. He scooted backward, trying clumsily to withdraw his knife from its sheath. A new scent hit Laszlo's nostrils: dried wolf blood. It was Zoltan's.

Laszlo's eyes flashed and a fierce growl buzzed in his throat. His ears flattened and his back arched.

"Back, Devil!" Père Raoul shouted, his voice trembling.

He managed to free his knife and waved it feebly in front of him. Laszlo's hackles rose. He bared his teeth and snapped viciously at the air.

The priest scooted back, edging right up to the bank, his bloody foot beyond the arc of the knife. Laszlo let out a hair-raising snarl. Père Raoul recoiled and, with no ground left behind him, toppled backward into the stream. As he hit the cold water his grip loosened and the knife disappeared beneath the waves. The trap on his foot snagged in a bush and moored him to the bank. He floated on his back, beating at the water with his arms, trying madly to keep his head above the surface. Laszlo knew that without help he would soon drown, and a part of him wanted nothing less. However, a larger part couldn't sit by and let it happen.

He reached out and snatched the priest's coattail in his teeth and tried pulling him back to shore. The bank, however, was too muddy; his hind paws could gain no traction. Instead of pulling the priest out, he was being pulled in. Soon he was in the water up to his jaw. He treaded water as best he could, but the current was very strong. It would have dragged him away had he not been biting down on the priest's coattail, had Père Raoul's foot not been anchored to the shore.

Soon, however, that anchor began to rip loose as the bush was slowly yanked up by the roots. The weight of the priest and the wolf together was too much. Laszlo considered letting go, but then realized that the priest's only hope for survival was to be released from the bank. The water wasn't deep for a man; he ought to be able to stand up in it and keep his head above water until Laszlo could get help. So Laszlo tugged harder at his coat until the bush ripped loose. It and the trap sank down to the muddy stream bottom. Père Raoul, now upright, tried to stand but the water was deeper than Laszlo had expected; it came up to the man's eyes. Again he was moored to the spot, again water filled his mouth and nose. He flailed and spluttered and Laszlo tried his best to drag him to safety, but he had no leverage against the weight of the trap. It struck him that maybe as a boy he could dive down and open the trap's jaws. He changed, his teeth still clinging to the priest's coat. Horrified, Père Raoul tried to scream, and ended up swallowing another mouthful of water.

Laszlo dove into the water — it was much colder without his fur — and followed the priest's coat down until he found the trap. He struggled with all his might to pry it open, but he didn't have the strength. Being human was no help. He swam back up.

"Don't worry!" he gasped as he broke through the surface. "I'll call my father! He'll help!"

He changed back to a wolf and paddled back to shore. There he howled for his father. Kalman answered immediately, as if he had been waiting for Laszlo to call. He was on his way.

When Laszlo turned back, he saw that the priest was floating face down in the stream. He was no longer struggling. He was motionless. Laszlo became a boy again and dove back into the water. There was still nothing he could do, but he could not just stand there on the bank and watch the man drown. He grappled again with the trap, to no avail. He resurfaced and tried again to pull the man to shore. It was futile, as was trying to lift him up above the surface of the waves. And then he saw that Père Raoul's eyes gaped open, wide and fixed, frozen in terror. They were the eyes of a dead man.

Laszlo looked away, up at the sky through the trees, and cried out. As he did, a large silver wolf dove into the stream and swam out to him. The wolf became his father, hooked his arm around Laszlo's chest, and pulled him back to shore.

CHAPTER THIRTEEN

Laszlo followed his father's footprints back toward the cave. He scented his mother first, then the sheep. Pernette had not yet given birth. He smelled Gizi, and he could hear her slow, labored breathing. And he smelled Muno. He wondered how she would greet the news of Père Raoul's death. Would she cheer? Would she grieve? It didn't seem like an occasion for either.

He thought about the priest's body, still anchored in the stream. Kalman had said it was better to leave him there, fearing if they dragged him onto the shore that animals would get at the body. The seigneur would surely send a search party and it would be better for the priest to be discovered drowned with the trap on his foot than feasted upon by wild beasts. It would make a wolf hunt less likely.

Still, knowing that the man was floating there, his life

departed, filled Laszlo with dread. Shouldn't he feel relieved, even glad, that Père Raoul was dead? He didn't. He felt worry and sorrow.

Rita was waiting by the cave entrance when they returned. They became human and she gathered them in her arms.

"Oh, thank God!" she breathed. "Thank God!"

Laszlo felt her body shiver with relief. Over her shoulder he saw Muno leaning against the white trunk of a birch tree. She held his cloak in his hand.

"Père Raoul is dead," he said to her. "Drowned. I tried to save him, but I . . ." He looked away. "I couldn't."

"Oh, Laszlo," Rita said. She released him and looked into his eyes. "How awful."

Muno raised a hand and set the heel of it on her forehead, as if her head had become so heavy it needed support. Her eyes lost their focus and grew red around the rims. She didn't say a word.

"When the men heard how many wolves there were in the woods, they became scared and fled," Kalman said. "In the rush, Père Raoul stepped into a trap and was left behind."

"I came upon him as a wolf," Laszlo said to Muno. "He was afraid and stumbled backward into a stream. The trap pulled him under. The water was so strong."

"It wasn't your fault, Laszlo," Rita said.

"The priest was not the only one to perish tonight," Kalman said somberly.

"Fridrik is dead, Laszlo," Rita said.

"Fridrik?" Laszlo gasped. It didn't seem possible. Laszlo knew that wolves were routinely killed by men. He knew that men went out in parties with the express purpose of killing as many of them as they could find. He knew also about the traps and poisons set out for them, some made in kitchens by women and set out by children. But this was Fridrik. Fridrik was a king, a lord of the woods. Lords are not destroyed like rats found in the grain. Fridrik was too dignified to be slaughtered so indiscriminately. The injustice of it roiled Laszlo's stomach.

"Père Raoul killed Zoltan, and Fridrik went into a rage," Kalman said. "He lunged at Père Raoul, and one of the village men shot him with an arrow."

Laszlo remembered the smell of blood on Père Raoul's knife, Zoltan's blood. Poor, rash Zoltan, struck down before he'd even grown into his paws.

"And Agnes?" Laszlo asked, afraid to hear the answer.

"She's in her nest," Rita said. "Safe, but mourning."

"Daniel and Klotild are with her," Kalman said. "But Aunt Rozsa is dead. She didn't stand a chance, as old as she was, and with a leg missing."

Laszlo could hear no more. He snatched up his cloak from Muno and wandered away toward the cave. He was after something reliable, something constant, something true. Gizi was lying in the cart, and Laszlo climbed in beside her. Her breathing rattled.

"It's me," he said, stroking her neck. "You'll be all right. You just need some rest."

◆　　◆　　◆

He was awakened hours later by Pernette. Muno was sitting up beside him in the cart.

"Is she delivering?" she whispered.

For a moment Laszlo didn't know where he was or why Muno was there. It was as if he'd awakened into some strange dream. Then, with too much clarity, it all came back to him.

"It sounds like it," he answered.

Pernette was outside the cave in a clump of saxifrage, lying on her side, protesting in long, low baas. A tiny foot, with a tiny hoof, was sticking out from between her legs.

"Stay back," Laszlo whispered to Muno. "She can do it herself."

Soon another foot appeared, then another, then a nose, and then the lamb slipped out, its fleece wet, its ears plastered to its head. Pernette stood and gave the call for the lamb to come to her, but it lay still on the ground. Laszlo rushed to it, pulled off his cloak, and began massaging the lamb with it. After a few seconds he stopped and checked for breathing. There was none, so he gave the lamb two hard slaps on the ribs. It sprang to life, scrambling up onto its wobbly legs, then promptly fell back onto its chin. Again it stood, and this time was able to hobble over to its mother, take a teat in its mouth, and begin to suckle.

"It's a ram," Laszlo said, peeking between its legs.

"I say we keep him anyway," Rita said. Laszlo turned to find his parents standing behind him. "It won't be long before we'll have to send Alphonse out to pasture."

Kalman nodded, then asked, "What will you name him, Laszlo?"

Laszlo thought a minute, then said, "Fridrik."

"Yes," Rita said, and, turning, dabbed away a tear with her knuckle.

To celebrate the birth, Laszlo retrieved the little wooden box from one of the sacks and offered everyone a chocolate. This time his parents accepted. The chocolate on Muno's tongue actually elicited a small smile, something Laszlo would not have thought possible.

◆　　◆　　◆

At dawn, Laszlo awoke with an unsettling feeling and knew at once what it meant. He set a trembling hand on Gizi's shoulder. Her body was cold. He shook her, and she did not shake like a living thing. Her head did not rock, her legs were as stiff as fallen branches. Her eyes had lost their moistness and become like glass. Gizi was not in the animal any longer. She had fled in the night.

Laszlo buried his face in her cords and tried not to cry. If he didn't cry, he thought, she wouldn't be dead. But he could not hold back the flow.

His crying woke his parents and they, too, wept for Gizi, and for their son's grief. Muno slipped away from them and sat on the ground with Pernette and her lamb, who were both bleating anxiously. Clearly the family's weeping was upsetting them. Muno rubbed little Fridrik's spongy new wool with her grimy fingers and told him over and over that everything would be all right, until at last the lamb took his mother's teat in his mouth and both ewe and lamb were calm.

Kalman lifted Gizi out of the cart and laid her on the ground on a blanket. Then he dug a hole, set her in it, and covered her over with dirt. Rita peeled off her tunic and fell forward. With a look to Muno, Kalman did the same. Laszlo changed, too, then the family howled their eulogy.

From the woods, more voices joined the mourning. Laszlo identified the howls of Daniel and Klotild, the surviving pups, and Agnes, clearly weakened from her labor and from woes of her own. Laszlo also heard Bertok, the lone wolf. It was clear from his tone that he had not only been accepted, but that he had also risen a notch in the pack's hierarchy. His voice seemed tuned to Klotild's, and Laszlo imagined that a new mateship had been formed. He was glad for Bertok, and glad for the surviving wolves. Père Raoul's men had cut off the pack's head, but had not killed it. It would continue.

◆　　◆　　◆

Pernette and her lamb rode in the cart with Muno when later the family set off. Alphonse deigned to walk, followed by Babette, whose wool was still coming out in handfuls, then Henriette, her udders red as beets, and, in the rear, Claudette. Once again, Kalman pulled; Rita and Laszlo pushed. Muno sat at the rear of the cart. No one said a word for hours as they plodded along the forest path.

It was Muno who finally broke the silence, asking Laszlo where they were headed. He told her about Marie-France's uncle and his offer of a home in Montcorbeau. He told her about the family's hopes for a friendlier village, and his heart felt lighter.

"Will Seigneur Pussort send anyone after us?" Laszlo asked his mother.

"I don't think so," Rita said. "They will certainly search for Père Raoul, but after last night it will not be easy to entice men back to the woods. If Seigneur Pussort does choose to pursue us, I doubt he will go as far as Montcorbeau. Seigneurs are usually only concerned with what falls within their own borders. I am certain that a few shepherds and a girl are not worth the trouble of a widespread search. My feeling is that they'll be content in having chased us off and will leave it at that."

"Of course you could be wrong, dear wife," Kalman said from the front. "The death of a priest is no small thing, and there is the prison guard, who can testify he was attacked by wolves in the dungeon."

"He was drunk," Rita said. "Who will believe him?"

"Those who want to," Kalman said.

"Well, maybe someone *will* show up in the new village," Rita said with a sigh. "But until they do, I for one am not going to fret about it."

"And so what about me?" Muno asked, looking down. "What's to be done with me?"

"You, my love, are one of us now," Rita said. "That is, if you want to be. I would like it very much if you would allow me to consider you my daughter. I've always wanted one."

Muno closed her eyes but, try as she might, could not hide her tears.

Laszlo smiled, comforted by the thought that she was now, in effect, his sister. It was now his right, if not his responsibility, to be concerned for her welfare, as it was now hers to watch out for him, her brother. He still felt other, less settled, emotions about Muno, emotions he did not fully understand. He had never in his life felt such a strong need to know that a person other than his parents was out of danger. He'd never felt toward anyone the intensity of feelings he had for Muno since first meeting her on the flushing. Those feelings remained within him; though, with Muno now a part of the family, they had changed. How, he couldn't say. Perhaps, he thought, it had been the not knowing how she was, along with her continually pushing him away, that had heightened his concern, that had caused him to think and worry about her so incessantly. Perhaps now, as his sister, she would no longer provoke such miserable preoccupation. He hoped so.

"Does this mean I'll become one, too?" Muno asked quietly.

"No," Rita said. "Sadly, it's not something one can choose to be. If more people could change, I think we'd be treated much more fairly. People would see then how lucky we are."

"It's true," Muno said. "You're not what people say you are. I wouldn't mind becoming like you. I'd prefer it to being human."

"There's nothing wrong with being human," Rita said, "just like there's nothing wrong with being a wolf, or a were-wolf, or even a rat. We are what we are born to be."

"'We must judge with more reverence the infinite power of nature,'" Kalman said, quoting Montaigne. "My father used to say that it does no good for a worm to wish it were a bird. A worm would do better to enjoy the mud and keep an eye on the sky."

"I'd rather be a bird than a worm," Laszlo said.

"That's the human being in you talking!" Rita laughed.

Laszlo laughed, too, and the grip of sadness in him loosened, if only momentarily. He did his best to savor that moment of laughter, to allow it to course through his body like a tonic, as the belladonna had once chased away his fever. There would be time, plenty of time, to worry about the future: whether it was wise or not for Muno to join a family of wolf folk, or even of Magyars; whether or not there

193

would be whispers about them in Montcorbeau. And there would be time to grieve for the past night's losses: for Gizi; for Fridrik, Zoltan, and Aunt Rozsa; and even for Père Raoul. For the moment, however, Laszlo wanted to keep all that at bay and bask in the happiness he felt, however fleeting, and in the warmth of the morning sun through the budding trees.

ACKNOWLEDGMENTS

First off, I'd like to thank the fourth-grade boy (sadly, I did not learn his name) who, six years ago, came into the public library where I was working and asked, "What does the *were* part of *werewolf* mean?" The answer was uninspiring (it's Old English for *man*); far more tantalizing was a sidebar in the children's dictionary we consulted, which described an old Greek myth of kindly shepherds transforming themselves into wolves in order to negotiate treaties with neighboring wolf packs.

After the boy left the library — and my circulation desk shift was complete — I began hunting for corroboration of this myth. I never found it, but in my search, I stumbled across another equally compelling werewolf story, this one hardly mythical and far from kindly; namely, that during the Inquisition, the Catholic Church and its agents tried, convicted, and executed thousands of men, women, and children for the crime of being werewolves. This bloody campaign was particularly virulent in France, where belief in — and fear of — werewolves was rampant. Between 1598 and 1600, one judge sent close to six hundred people to their deaths, many of them at the stake.

From these two wildly different tales — one pastoral, the other tragic; one mythical, the other appallingly true — sprang a third. For that, I have to thank a fourth grader and a dictionary, two things one should never underestimate.

I also wish to acknowledge here my debt to the many authors whose works were invaluable to me during my research, several of whom deserve special mention. Chief among these is Pierre Goubert, whose book, *The French Peasantry in the 17th Century* (Cambridge University Press, 1986), provided ample details, wryly given, on the grueling daily life of French peasants (which, as Goubert notes, was not as rustically romantic as we Americans, with our distressed wooden furniture and peasant breads, are inclined to imagine). Also noteworthy, and disarming, are Margaret Bradbury's *The Shepherd's Guidebook* (Rodale Press, 1977) and Adelaide L. J. Gosset's *Shepherds of Britain: Scenes from Shepherd Life Past and Present, From the Best Authorities* (B. Blom, 1972; originally published in 1912). I have Ms. Bradbury to thank for Kalman's delightful "tuft-of-wool"

excuse. Two books on wolves to which I repeatedly retu.
were Barry Lopez's eloquent *Of Wolves and Men* (Scribner.
1978) and Peter Steinhart's incisive *The Company of Wolves*
(Knopf, 1995). And credit should be given to the *Eclogues* of
Virgil and the *Essais* of Montaigne. I read selections from
each frequently during the writing of this story in a desperate attempt at stealing some of their *joie de vivre*. Perhaps not
coincidentally, both works make mention of werewolves.

More personally, I'd like to tender my deepest apprecia-
tion to the ever-helpful staffs of the Copper Queen and Port
Townsend libraries, and also to Joy Kaplan (the knitter),
Jennifer Turney (the shepherd), Marcia Adams (the shearer),
Brigitte Berg (the translator), Gabriel Cohen (the trumpeter),
and as always, to Alice (the booklover), *merci beaucoup*.